# Snowed In at the Cabin

# Snowed In at the Cabin

### K.P. KNUPP

Copyright © 2026 by K.P. Knupp

ISBN: 979-8-9932255-1-7 (Paperback)

ISBN: 979-8-9932255-0-0 (e-book)

Edited by: Tanisha (@fantasybooksandbudgets), Mish (@Tht.Book.Girl), and Kristen Susienka

Internal illustrations by Marta Riva of Into The Forest @marta.intotheforest

Full page designs by MgsDesiigns

Cover design by: Miblart



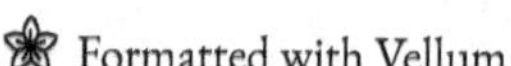 Formatted with Vellum

**The Witch's Curse**

Rachel's curse is nothing new. She's dealt with it her entire life. One day every year filled with bad luck.

But when Caleb, a handsome wizard ,comes to town, things start getting worse than ever before. Spilled coffee is one thing. But when her magic starts backfiring and a seers premonition looms overhead, it's time to dig deeper for a cure.

Rachel and Caleb have one day to unravel the curse, or risk it becoming worse than they could ever imagine.

**Mistletoe and Wayward Spells**

Becks is overjoyed at the thought of going to Candy Cane Lane, the biggest Christmas event in the state of Massachusetts. Until the sight of mistletoe and kissing couples makes her want to use her fire magic to burn all of the tiny plants to dust.

Instead, she decides to craft a spell eradicating all mistletoe from the town. Only, the spell takes a turn and multiplies them three fold. And what's worse? The attractive tree farmer wizard informs Becks of an old town superstition. If one finds themselves under the mistletoe and refuses a kiss, they'll be cursed for eternity. Great. More curses.

**This Mess We Live In**

Through the various degrees of life we experience love and pain. To be able to experience it at all is a blessing, but at times it still hurts. While new love can light you up again.

This is for the healing journey. For the fear of the unknown and how diving in can often times be the only answer.

There's brightness on the other side, you just have to keep going.

**Fade**

Ali doesn't know if she's going crazy, or if what she's feeling is real. There's a presence trying to get her attention, but what happens when she decides to believe.

# Contents

*We never know when the end will come for us,*
*so take that risk,*
*Leave the job you hate,*
*Fall in love,*
*And always chase your dreams.*
*If not now, when?*

*This life is worth living, now.*

# PART
## One

# CHAPTER 1

## *Alexandra*

APPROXIMATELY TWO MINUTES after the worst interview I've ever experienced, my palms are practically dripping with sweat. I'm freaking out. My boss, Bill Murphy, and his right hand, Dan Balding haven't stopped staring at the papers in front of them. The ones that say whether or not they believe I'm the right candidate for the coveted position I've applied for. Shit. It doesn't feel like the fourth time in two years is the charm.

"Alexandra, off the record, of course. What do you hope to accomplish by moving up within Johnson Enterprise? Do you not enjoy the work you do as a secretary?" Dan scratches his fingers through the patchy beard he's been trying to grow for the last three months. The hair still hasn't filled in on his cheeks and part of his chin, and it makes him look like a balding cat.

I wipe my hands on my pants again and slide them both a copy of my design mock-up for a made-up brand we could work with. "I have fresh ideas and would like to utilize my design capabilities within this new role as the associate designer. I believe I could take our designs to the next level and increase our client workload by over thirty percent." I slide another design along with demographics to them. "I constantly watch trends to keep up with the market and hone my skills. I'm eager to learn more and help the company."

I started here fresh out of high school and worked my way through college while learning every nook and cranny of Johnson Enterprise. Years of sleepless nights, early mornings, and weekends packed with studying for my art and design degree while working my butt off have apparently amounted to nothing. Mom always said if I was going to go for a useless degree like art I had to pay for it myself, which made me that much more determined to prove her wrong.

After I finished my degree three years ago, I enrolled in marketing courses in the evenings. I'm determined to make my way in this corporate world. This is the fourth promotion I've interviewed for in the last two years, but they keep finding reasons to keep me in my place. This company is starting to feel like a dead end, and if they won't see my worth, I'll have to claw myself out.

Bill slides the designs to his stack without a second glance. "We love your ambition, but at this time you just don't have enough experience. I would like to see you take on additional tasks within the company while keeping up with your current work-load, to show you're serious about moving up." He sighs and sets his hands on his protruding stomach, his mouth turning up in a small smile. "We just feel that our other option is a better fit. Maybe you could get the next opening or possibly the one a few years out to give you more time to grow your skills."

Dan smirks, and I stifle the urge to scream. I already take on work in multiple departments and stay later than anyone else every night to make sure the next day runs smoothly. They know this. They sign my time cards.

I bite my cheek. "Can I just ask...is Clay the other candidate?" I grab my notebook and slide the chair back.

Bill clears his throat. "Again, off the record." I incline my head, so he will continue. "Yes. He's proven to be more than capable with the delegation of tasks and making it a point to come to gatherings outside of work hours." My face feels like it's on fire. Clay has only been here for six months and has no design background, but he *does* go out every night with Dan and Bill to the bar to mingle and hit on chicks, or so I'm told every morning when he rolls in late sporting a large black coffee and wearing his sunglasses.

I'm about to stand and walk out like the good employee I am, but I can't help myself. I'm so fed up with being passed over again and again that my anger gets the best of me, letting my mouth fly freely. "If you don't mind, what qualifications does Clay have over me? I feel like I've more than proven myself in the eight years I've been here, putting in endless hours and taking on a multitude of work in various departments." I hold my composure as I scream in triumph inside for finally saying something.

Bill chuckles. "No offense, *honey*, but we just don't see the leadership capabilities that are required for this position. Take a look at Clay. He's able to delegate more of his work to others to free up more time for useful things like working lunches with Dan and me at The Grill. Taking the time to sit with higher–ups and shmooze them really helps a guy stand out, you know. He's a big team player by not trying to tackle it all on his own, which allows him to finish work early. Delegating shows he can take on a larger workload without staying late or pushing the need for another employee. He saves us money this way, you see?"

Dan is feeding off this bro energy and jumps in. "You're *so* right, Bill. I mean, at the end of the day, the work still gets done, so who cares who actually does it? You have the same opportunities Clay does, so *really*, it's your own choice to stay late and shoulder everything alone."

I nod, but I can't stand this anymore. Are they serious? Because I get more work done, I'm the problem? I help the departments that Clay dumps his work on, so it does get done on time and the customers don't suffer, but he's the one rewarded. "Thank you for your time today, but given this new information, I quit. I'll email my formal letter on Monday."

I push through the doors and make my way to my

desk and rip my purse from the file drawer. I start to throw the photos of me and my sister into my bag along with my favorite pens and notepad.

Austin jumps up from his cubicle next to mine. "Hey, what's going on?"

"I quit." I throw my pink Bluetooth keyboard and mouse in my overflowing purse before I hike it over my shoulder.

"Damn! I'm proud of you, babes. I wish I could quit. What are you going to do now?" He drums his painted fingernails on the edge of the cubical. We chat every day about life and the endless bullshit this place throws at us, so honestly, it's no surprise to him.

"I have no idea yet. I'll let you know where I land, so you can ditch out too." I start walking backwards. I can't be here anymore.

Austin gives me a salute. "Deal. Stay brave. I expect to hear from you in a month at the latest."

"God, I hope it doesn't take that long. Talk soon." I wave and rush to the elevator.

My heart is pounding so loud I can barely make out Bill calling my name from the meeting room. I don't stop. I just power through, I don't want to be guilted into staying, or second guess my choices. I need air and away from Johnson Enterprise. My meeting was set for the end of the day, so I told Taylor, my boyfriend of three months, that I didn't know how long it would be and planned to get drinks with my best friends Ashlyn and Jaz after. But after this shit-show, I just want to go home and be in my sweatpants. Maybe I can get Taylor to give me that massage he promised.

*That would be nice.*

As long as he's not too busy working. He also works at a marketing firm, but he just started when we got together. We met at a convention. He was trying to land a new job after finishing his degree, and I was there to hand out fliers for Johnson Enterprise. We bonded over the fact that we were both workaholics and wanted to move up in the business. It works in our relationship because we don't get mad when we have to work late, or if I'm too exhausted to go out, especially after grinding for the last eight years of my life.

I send a text to the group chat with my friends.

> Alexandra: Well, it was shit, and I decided to freak out and quit! Full panic mode now, so tonight will have to be rescheduled. Love you!

> Ashlyn: They never deserved you! But I require deets soon!

> Jaz: Their loss! Tomorrow? Class got canceled. Teacher has some vacation or something?

> Ashlyn: I'm down!

> Alexandra: ... Fine. Bring donuts.

> Jaz: YES! Done <3

I open the dreaded thread to my mom and send her a

quick text to let her know I didn't get the promotion. Again. I set my phone to silent. I know she will be disappointed and blow up my phone about new exciting men she wants to set me up with. She doesn't get that I'm not looking for a handout husband. I like working for what I have.

The drive home is a blur, my mind is white noise on max volume. I pull into my parking spot at my apartment complex, not really sure how I made it here in one piece, but choosing to ignore it. I grab my overflowing purse and fling my car door open, ready to be done with today. I slam my door a little too aggressively and run through the main door of the building with the white noise in my head still taking over my senses. But as I swing into the lobby, my body bounces off a hard chest. I stumble, drop my purse to save myself from falling on my ass, and watch in slow motion as its contents scatter in every direction like marbles bouncing off a polished floor.

*Great. Just great.*

My face feels like it's on fire. "Sorry," I mumble

without looking up. I bend down to grab my stuff and toss everything back into my bag as fast as I can. The quicker I can get inside to hide, the better.

"No worries. I'm often in my own mind. I'll help," he says.

Ugh I know that voice. Fucking Clay.

*Kill me now.* "It's okay, really. I can get it." I'm going to crawl in a hole and die. I do not need his smug face anywhere near me today.

Clay's laugh is like nails on a chalkboard. "I've seen you in various positions living in the same building for the last two years, remember?"

I snatch the last of my tampons and throw them in the bag. "Don't remind me." He starts to talk again, but I jump up and skip three stairs at a time to get the hell away from him. He walked up on me and the girls at the apartment pool last summer and hasn't stopped talking about our bodies since. Such a child.

I make it up the thirty-two steps to my apartment—yes, I've counted—because there's no elevator and it sucks. Digging through my purse, I finally find my keys buried under everything else. I sigh. *Finally I can just relax.* I open my door and hear a scream, making me jump.

"Yes! Yes! Right there, TayTay!" A slap follows, and the woman screams again.

I'm in shock. What the actual fuck is happening and why today? I march down the hallway to the living room, my keys still in my hand as I take in the trail of clothes on the floor and the sound of bodies slapping together.

*Maybe it's porn on the TV. Who knows? Right, and the clothes just came out of the screen. Idiot.*

I see the blonde hair cascading down the side of my couch first. Taylor grunts as he slams into her from behind. "You like that, baby?"

Great. As if my day could get any worse. What a dick. You'd think three months together would at least mean he could dump me before screwing someone else. Or at least do it in his own shitty apartment.

I drop my purse loudly on the floor and start clapping. "Yes, baby. I love it so much."

He pulls out and grabs his dick. Like I haven't seen it before. "Shit. What are you doing here?"

"I live here. I pay the rent." I roll my eyes and scream, "GET THE FUCK OUT OF MY APARTMENT!" Jesus fucking Christ.

"What does she mean her apartment?" The blonde is slowly putting her clothes on like she didn't just ruin my already shitty day.

"Nothing. Look, I thought you were going out tonight?" Taylor is still standing in the middle of my living room holding himself, not moving to get his clothes. Does he think I'm going to let him finish? "This doesn't mean anything. I just had a rough day and needed a release. We can talk about this. Don't be hostile."

I whip his shitty underwear and pants at him. "Get. The. Fuck. Out." I'm fuming. My vision is blacking out on the edges.

"Seriously?" His mouth turns up in a sneer as he puts his pants on.

I go to the door and start chucking their remaining clothes and shoes into the hallway.

The blonde starts screaming. "Those shoes are worth more than your apartment, you bitch! It's freezing out there!"

I feel my mouth turn up in a smile, but my emotions are turned off at this point. I can't deal with this shit. "Dead serious," I say to Taylor as I snatch the key I gave him off the counter and slide it into my pocket.

I ignore the blonde bimbo. She can figure it out herself. Shouldn't fuck a guy in another girl's apartment in early winter.

Taylor grabs the blonde's hand, pulling her to the hall to get their clothes off the floor. "I don't know why you're acting like this. I have needs and you've been too busy..."

"We both work the same grueling hours, or at least I thought we did." I sneer at him, "Forget I exist." I slam the door in his face, cutting off his garbage excuses. I can't listen to this shit. I'm going to have to burn my couch. After pulling out my phone, I send a message to the group chat.

Alexandra: Come over. Bring a lighter and two bottles of wine!

Ashlyn: What happened?

Alexandra: Taylor fucked some blonde bitch on my couch, so we have to get rid of it…now!

Ashlyn: Fuck! I'll be right there!

Jaz: I'll get the wine!

# CHAPTER 2
## James

RYDER COMES BARRELING through my office door, not bothering to knock, as usual. "You won't believe who wants a meeting."

"Yeah, sure. Come on in. I'm not busy." I lean away from the contract I've been drafting for the last hour and give my younger cousin my full attention.

He doesn't acknowledge I've spoken as he continues, too caught up in his excitement. "The CEO of Kemp Global! Can you believe it? Kemp never reaches out to anyone and they haven't used an advertising firm since they started up three years ago and grew into an overnight success. If we can land them as clients, it will be huge for our reach." He stops pacing, and collapses into the chair across from me, running his hands through his short blond hair. He's right. Kemp Global started with wine and spirits, exploding with the younger generation. The amount of social media coverage they get for free is insane. If we put our logo with theirs, it would be a huge boost for our visibility with our other clients. Not to mention the amount we charge for a year of services for a company that big.

I steeple my hands together, pressing them to my chin. "When's the meeting?"

The smirk crossing his face makes me regret my question. "Tonight. Club X. The CEO is young and known to be a wild card, so we have to play this right. You're going to have to pretend you like to go out on the weekends and party. You know, so he believes you actually like his product."

I feel my eyebrows touch my hair line. "Ryder, I'm thirty years old and ready to settle down. I don't like to go out and party. You couldn't get him to come here? Where it's quiet, and we can get him to sign a contract?"

"Right, but no one has to know that our leader is a grandpa. And no. I tried, but he insists the company in charge of his marketing has to understand his demographic. Thus, we go to Club X, where every young person parties on the weekends." He rolls his eyes, grabs the stapler off my desk, and throws it in the air just to catch it and do it again. I swear this kid can't sit still.

I say kid, but we're the same age. Even our other cousin, Alester, is only a few months older. Our moms were as close as you could get. After mine passed away when I was five, my two aunts made sure to keep me close and be my bonus moms as best they could. The three of us have been equally as inseparable since we were young. Living in the same neighborhood meant we could just rotate houses for dinner every night. Especially when it was just me and Dad. Aunt Alice and Aunt Andrea wanted to keep an eye on us. For Mom. Then Dad got sick when I was in high school, and in the first year of college everything went downhill fast.

With everything I've been through, it feels like we are in completely different times of our lives. Ryder goes out almost every night and brings women home every chance he can get–never the same one twice–and never in his bed, only the spare room or the woman's house if he can get away with it. Honestly, even when I was like him, I wasn't as bad as he is. With everything that happened with my dad and then my disaster of an engagement almost five years ago now, I'm over all the drama. I enjoy a quiet life besides having Ryder around.

"Helllllloooo, James!" Ryder waves his hand in my face.

I sigh. "Yes. Fine, we can go, but I'm not staying late. I'll greet him, introduce the company, and then you can take over while I go home." *And relax in my quiet empty apartment.*

I caved and got a penthouse in a new development with top-of-the-line appliances and marble countertops throughout, mostly because Alester insisted that the CEO of a company and someone with my bank account shouldn't live in a regular apartment. Even though that's exactly what I wanted to do. I wouldn't compromise on location, though. I needed it to be close to the office, even with Thomas driving me where I need to go. I'd rather not waste time on commuting.

Ryder and Alester are in the same building a floor down, each with half the floor, so we can ensure our privacy. Alester also installed top-of-the-line security cameras and transformed one of his spare rooms into a giant surveillance station. There are so many monitors in there it looks like a news station.

"Alester can draft the documents for Kemp to sign there," I tell Ryder. "We don't want a repeat of the last time you took out a client only to let it all burn to the ground before you went home." Why Kemp's CEO, Patrick, has to have a meeting in a loud club still doesn't make sense to me, but we built our company on making everything easier for the client. So, if he wants the club, we go to the club.

Ryder cringes and holds his hands up in surrender. "It's not my fault his girl wanted me! She was grown and chose to take a dip on the wild side without asking her boyfriend if he was okay with an open relationship."

I scoff and shake my head. "It wasn't an open relationship. That's the problem. We don't need to lose this client before we even sign. So, get him to sign before you do anything stupid." I wave him away. "I'll fill in Alester. You go get whatever work it is you actually do here. I need to check on the property before I meet you at the club."

Ryder chuckles, sets my stapler back in its place, and

heads out of my office towards the lounge. *Idiot. Does he ever work?*

I send a few emails before logging off and stuffing documents in my briefcase to work on in the car. I text Thomas to be ready in five. He's the best investment I've made going into this company. I can continue to work during the commute, to meetings, or while traveling around town, and he gets a nice salary for his family. I hate wasting time on anything in my life. Time is short, and I can't afford to use it wistfully on work or personal life. I wish I had found out earlier about my ex fiancé Rebecca and all of her schemes, but I guess that's how you learn life lessons.

By the time I hit the lobby, Thomas has the SUV idling at the curb and my door propped open. He's the easiest person in the company to work with. He keeps his past to himself, being a retired Army vet, but he's always on time and never questions what I need. I nod to him as I slide into the back seat. "Thomas, how's lining up the piano lessons for Jessica? She just turned twelve, right?"

Thomas shuts the door and makes his way to the driver's side before answering. "She starts next week and is overjoyed with the piano you gifted her." His eyes shine in the rearview mirror, and I have to look down at my paperwork.

"It was nothing. What about Annie? She wanted to start some sort of self-defense class? Did she figure out which one?" I ask, leaning back in my seat when Thomas pulls onto the main road. His eyes stay glued ahead of him.

"Ah, yes. She chose MMA. My little five-year-old wants to jump right in the ring." He chuckles. "Seems I will have my work cut out for me with these girls."

I smirk. He jokes, but I know his family means everything to him.

"Well, let me know if she needs anything. Access to training facilities or gear. It's no problem." He's a great man and deserves to enjoy his family time without worrying about anything financial when it comes to them.

He inclines his head but doesn't fully acknowledge the offer. I'll have to let Alester know to keep a digital eyeball on them, to see when they need anything. It's the easiest way to know what our employees need, especially when they feel an unnecessary guilt in telling one of us. We make it very clear that we love taking care of our employees. They're like family, and we want to know what activities or events they're into so we can gift them things occasionally. Because what's the point of having all this money if I can't spend it on people I care about? I don't need to horde it. I have plenty–hell even more than plenty–to live well within my means. I have the acreage, apartments near every office, a couple vacation homes, plus I give back to charities, and there's nothing wrong with spoiling my employees too. This is why they don't like me in the media. They want dirt, but I don't care enough to give it to them.

"Where to today?" Thomas asks as we head down main street.

"The acreage. I need to check a few things, then we have to go to the club for a meeting." I pause. "It will be brief."

Thomas merges onto the ramp out of town when I have an idea. "Actually, let's stop by the bookstore first." He seamlessly changes lanes to head in the opposite direction as I pick up my phone and dial.

"Endlessly Books! This is Kayla. How can I help you?"

"Hi Kayla. I'm going to be at your store in twenty-five minutes. I'd like you all to put together a large quantity of books and toys for a variety of ages of children. Price does not matter. I'm just on a time crunch and can't gather everything myself. As much as you can pick out in that time is perfectly fine."

"Uh. Okay. Any amount we can gather you said? Are you sure?" Kayla's voice drags out, her nervousness radiating through the phone.

"I'm sure. Your store manager knows me. Tell him Mr. Edward will be there soon." I hang up without waiting for the young girl to respond.

I pull out my packet of applications to flip through them while I wait to arrive at the bookstore. There are a lot of positions to fill at our new location, and finding the perfect candidate takes time.

"We are here, sir," Thomas says as he shifts the vehicle into Park.

I sigh. "Thomas, I asked you not to call me that. James is perfectly fine."

He chuckles. "Sorry, James. I've been around a long time. Some habits are hard to break."

He climbs out and rounds the SUV to open my door. I stuff my papers into my briefcase and nod my thanks. Thomas likes everything the traditional way, and I try my best not to force change on him too often. I let him get the door each time, but I'm trying to break the sir comments. They make me feel pretentious.

"Thanks, Thomas. I'll be right back out." I jog up to the building since I'm on a time crunch. When I open the door, the store manager is there to greet me. "Mark, good to see you," I say. "I take it you got my message."

"Yes, yes, Mr. Edward. I have everything right around the corner here and it's all rung up the way you like. It's ready for payment whenever you are." I round the corner to the cash register at the end of the long counter and swipe my card without looking. The machine starts spitting out the receipt. It takes a full minute for it to finish. Mark neatly folds the yard-long slip of paper and hands it to me.

"Thank you. Do you have someone who can help me get it to the SUV, or should I ring my driver?" I ask.

"Not to worry. I have it all handled." He waves two male employees over, and they start pulling two long carts stacked with ten boxes on each cart that are overflowing with books and toys.

*Perfect.*

"These two are going to follow you out and load everything inside for you." Mark extends his hand, so I reach out and shake it. "Thank you so much for your business."

"Thank you for your speedy service. The children are going to love everything," I say, and he beams up at me.

This is by far my favorite part of having seemingly endless funds. Being able to buy things for children in shelters and orphanages. It may seem small on my account, but to them, it's a bright spot in their day. The older ones can have new books to escape into, and the smaller kids get beginner books and stuffed animals. I started having the store throw games in the boxes too, for variety. It doesn't feel like I'm doing enough for the kids, but seeing Avery, the blonde three-year-old's face light up when she grabs a new stuffy and a book has me coming back as often as I can.

It doesn't take long for the employees to load the SUV, then Thomas pulls back onto the road towards the Boys and Girls Harbor. It's a short drive before Thomas winds up the gravel drive, parks, and makes his way to my door.

A volunteer rushes to our vehicle.

"Can I help you?" she asks.

I gesture to the trunk and Thomas clicks it open. "I have some donations for the kids."

Her shoulders relax. "That's amazing. I'll get a dolly and we can take it to the lunch room, but the children are all on a field trip right now."

"That's fine. I'll see them next time."

She takes off for the dolly, so we can unload everything.

After taking five loads of boxes back and forth, we are back on the road and heading out of the city.

Since we decided to add this new expansion, I always have more paperwork to do and applications to go over. I pull out my laptop and get to work as Thomas drives the half hour out of the city to the acreage. I originally bought the property for my dad. He was the one who suggested the first company we signed with while he was sick in the hospital. I thought we were going to have more time together than we did, so I wanted him to have a nice place to finish out his days. We unfortunately didn't get much time, so now it sits empty.

As we pull up the long driveway lined with trees for privacy, I take in the fifty acres of land with cattle moving through the trees and creek, some huddled in the barn for warmth. Northern Minnesota is nice this time of year, right before the snow falls. I don't mind the small city of Shadowbrook. It's growing quickly, so it's the perfect spot for us to plant our expansion. I just prefer being in the middle of nowhere. The silence of the country gives my mind a break. I can just exist for a while.

Thomas parks in front of the garage, his eyes meet mine in the mirror, filled with sympathy, but he doesn't say anything. I look away, pull the handle, and climb out.

I go to the front door, unlocking it and stepping through when a memory takes over.

*I walk into the house and smell the fresh pot of coffee brewing. "Dad? Where are you?"*

*"Living room, setting the TV up for the big race later."*

*I smile to myself, thinking of my dad back when he raced dirt bikes, before the diagnosis. Before they told him he had stage four genetic lung cancer, and they didn't know how long had left. He was the only sixty-year-old I knew who would still jump on a bike and race around the track in the summer, but he loved it. It didn't matter what place he got the last few years; he just loved being out there in his gear. That had to stop when he found out about the cancer and began treatments. He's been making the most of his time, and he loves being out in this new home with cattle to look after.*

*I pay a ranch hand to do any manual labor and keep up on the day to day, so Dad can do what he's able and still enjoy it out here. A nurse comes daily to check on anything else he needs and make sure his meds are laid out and marked for when he needs them. Otherwise, he keeps himself busy, walking every day, grilling in the summer, and watching his show or dirt bike races. He's not as active as he used to be, but he's here.*

*I check the fridge on the way to the living room and make a note to have someone do a grocery run and meal prep healthier meal options for him.*

*In the living room he's prepping his big chair with an*

extra blanket. His side table has a few electrolyte drinks, protein bars, and a bowl of popcorn.

"You look like you're ready to not move for a few hours," I say.

He looks up from messing with the remote, his face breaking into a smile. "My boy! I am ready. Have you seen the kids set to get into the qualifiers? It's going to be a wild race–lots of money on the line." He walks towards me and pulls me into a hug. "I've missed you. You've been busy. Have you met a lady yet?" He wiggles his eyebrows at me.

I chuckle, trying to ignore the fact that he's more skin and bones lately. "No, just busy with work. You know I don't have time for women right now."

We walk to the kitchen, and he pours us both a cup of coffee and slides a blueberry muffin towards me.

He takes a sip, watching me over his mug. "You know you'll have to slow down eventually and enjoy life, or you'll end up alone on your death bed."

I give him a look. "You're not alone on your death-bed."

He throws his head back and lets out a deep belly laugh. "I know! You've staffed me with a hot young nurse who always checks on me, and half the time another young lady comes with groceries. I had the love of my life already. That was enough for me. I'm not worried about me; I also have you. You're everything to me. I just worry that you're working too much. You haven't taken the time to actually enjoy life." He really looks at me then, pulling me in. "I've lived a long full life. I went to all the places I wanted to. I *have enjoyed living and seeing the world. You haven't lived outside of work. You barely experienced a year of college before you moved onto building your company, which I'm proud of, but if you're traveling, it's for work. I think you should take time off soon and do something for you. That's all."*

*I scratch the back of my neck, trying to avoid agreeing with him because he's not wrong. But he picks up his mug and turns back to the living room. "Come on. Let's sit and watch the pre-races for a little bit before you leave for work again."*

*I shake off his comments and make my way to the chair next to his, my coffee and muffin in hand. I need to come out here more and spend time with him before anything happens. I can always travel later. My time with him is limited, but I don't like being the one to remind him of it.*

*We sit and watch motocross together for an hour, talking about all the new riders, before I have to head back into town.*

Now I walk around the empty house, imagining him here in his chair, smiling. I continue to have people come take care of the house when I can't be here, but it's not the same.

I tap the counter, ready to leave again. I've seen enough. Made sure the place is still standing. I could listen when the people I pay tell me the house is fine, but there's something about coming and seeing it for myself. It's too lonely out here for me to stay, but one day I might. Having a nice place my dad would enjoy was one of the main selling points, but we both knew he wouldn't last forever. I created the design in a way I knew he would enjoy, but I also set it up to be my home base away from work.

I lock up the house and climb in the backseat again. As we drive back down the driveway, another memory from that day with Dad floods my mind.

*Dad waves from the wrap-around porch, his big smile still stuck to his face.*

He loved the porch. He would get up early and drink his morning coffee out there. He said that mom would have loved it, and it reminded him of her every time he watched the sunrise with his coffee. The same way they would have done if she hadn't died when I was young. They were madly in love, and dad never wanted to marry again. He had a few ladies in town he spent time with–some used to come and visit him during the week–but they all knew he wouldn't settle down again.

I check my watch and let out a sigh. "I won't have time to go home before the meeting, so we will just have to go straight to the club. I'm sure Ryder is already there."

"Yes, sir," Thomas says and tries to hide his smirk, but he's been with the family long enough that he knows exactly how all three of us operate. I ignore the 'sir' this time. He's trying to break it, but he's from a different generation that shows respect with their words.

I pull open my laptop again so I can continue working. Getting this new location up and fully functioning in Shadowbrook is our top priority. Our other locations in New York and California have all the employees necessary so we don't need to micromanage them, which allows us to expand to the Midwest, where we're from. Ryder, Alester, and I had always wanted to create a home base here, especially with the acreage. We just couldn't do it as fast as we wanted.

The three of us got into New York University straight out of high school. I wanted to do business and marketing, Alester settled on computer science and programming, and Ryder went for accounting and economics. We knew then that we would eventually create a business together. We just needed to figure out *what type* of business.

During the end of our first year, Dad got really sick. I flew back home to be with him, continuing my projects online. Dad gave us that first company to reach out to. With him dying in the hospital, I didn't want to be states away, so I deferred the rest of my program, pitched the idea to my cousins, and we decided to give it a shot. Marketing for large companies, working with artists to create one-of-a-kind material agencies couldn't find anywhere else, and connecting them with other businesses that aligned with their ideas took off like a forest fire.

Family Farms was our first company out of Minnesota that we signed. That check allowed me to get the acreage for Dad outside of Shadowbrook, but closer to Faith, Minnesota. And set up our small hub in rural

New York, so we could keep our connections and grow within a large marketing location. When Dad passed, I didn't need to fly back and forth to Minnesota anymore, so I went deep into gaining clients.

We set our sights on California to find small up-and-coming companies that wanted to invest in themselves and us. I worked around the clock, hiding from my grief and building our empire into what it is today, but it became exhausting. Alester and Ryder wanted our next location to be closer to where we all grew up. Faith, Minnesota, is too small of a town for a marketing company, but there are plenty of cities nearby for our work to succeed. I knew I needed to face my dad's ghost of memories, so here we are. Building a base near where it all started. Faith is where Ryder and Alester's families are. About two hours from Shadowbrook. It's a small town where everyone knows everyone, and you could spend the day walking through downtown enjoying all the small businesses. It's full of sympathetic smiles when they see me, so I've avoided it for the last eight years as much as possible.

Lost in my head, I shake myself out of my thoughts and glance from the window to my computer. I shoot a couple of more promising applications over to Ryder and Alester as we pull up to the club.

*How did so much time pass already?*

I close my computer and slide it into my bag, ready to get this over with.

The bass from inside the building is vibrating the

vehicle. I rub my hands over my eyes and glance up at Thomas. "I won't be long. Stay somewhat close, but get a nice dinner."

He chuckles at me as I slide out of the vehicle, not giving him a chance to come around, and make my way inside. He never listens to me about the dinner, but I wouldn't mind. I could always go for a long walk to clear my mind. Stop thinking about work for half a second.

Sometimes that scares me, though, because if I'm not thinking about work, I'm probably going to start thinking about one of the hardest days of my life.

# CHAPTER 3

## *Alexandra*

ASHLYN IS BARRELING through the door before I can get it fully open. You'd think she was the one being cheated on with how hard she shoulder-checks my door. Her silver dress with heels clicking across my floor promises trouble.

"I can't believe the nerve of that asshole!" she roars. "Who does he think he is? He's not even that good looking to be going after more than one woman at a time!" She flings her hand behind her. "I picked up Jaz on the way."

She's rambling, so I lean against the counter and let her have it.

"We're all going out." Ashlyn continues. "I'm calling in the 6-1-1. No excuses. You go where I say."

The 6-1-1 is a rule we made up when we became friends. In case of an emergency, one friend can call upon the code, ensuring the others follow, no matter what. It works best when dealing with introverted friends.

Jaz hangs back, leaning against the wall near the doorway while holding the bottles of wine I had requested. Her black hair hangs in loose curls down her back and almost matches her leather jacket and jeans. Black is her signature color, and she looks damn good in it.

I look down at my oversized hoody and yoga pants with fluffy socks, feeling underdressed. Especially since I am ready to binge New Girl in my room with my best friends given the couch is untouchable.

*Ugh.* I loved that couch. Now I have to go shopping for a new one. My head snaps to the ceiling as I wonder how I got so lucky to have to deal with this shit.

I glance back at Ashlyn and sigh when she snaps her fingers at me. "Fine, whatever," I say. "I'll go under two conditions." Before she can jump in and say the 6-1-1 allows for no conditions, I continue, "One, we get rid of this plague-infested couch first. And two, I'm not changing."

Their heads swivel between each other and back to me with wide eyes.

"I'm going in this. I don't need to attract attention tonight like you." I flourish my hand towards Ashlyn's entire being. "With your gorgeous body in that glittery silver thing you call a dress with those insane heels. And you," I point at Jaz, "looking all cool and mysterious. I'm just going to have a drink or five and forget the name Taylor."

Jaz is shaking trying to hide her laugh behind her hand, while Ashlyn looks at me with a devilish grin that makes me groan internally. "Who said we were going to a bar?"

"Oh no," I groan. "Not the club."

Ashlyn comes over and squeezes me tight, then looks at me with puppy dog eyes.

*Ugh.* "Fiiine. Let me get my shoes." *And get out of these fuzzy socks…No one wants sweaty toes.*

Jaz's chuckle echoes from the doorway. "Cool. Well, I'm going to do a round in your building, see if there's any guys walking around I can talk into moving that thing." She nods at the offending couch. "I don't want to mess up my nails." She slides the bottles on the counter before heading out the door.

I raise an eyebrow at Ashlyn, but she shrugs. "You know she'll find someone. She always does."

Fifteen minutes later, three guys are sliding the couch into some guy's first-floor apartment. I refused to touch the thing.

Jaz made it halfway down the hall before running into a group of guys carrying a case of beer and a couple pizzas towards an apartment a few doors down. One of those men knew a guy on the first floor who'd just moved in after his first semester of college. Dorm life supposedly didn't suit him. I told him it was free as-is, and he didn't question it. Not my job to tell him other things happened on it.

Jaz is our quiet, mostly innocent friend, always buried deep in graduate research. Ashlyn is our wild child. She comes from a rich family that gives her love in the form of an unlimited black card, so she found her own family…us. I guess I'm the artist. Well, an artist without a job now, but hopefully an artist who can make a living off of it soon. Or I'll be looking for someone to crash with.

Now that my living room is basically empty without my amazing but tainted couch, I give it one last glance as my shoulders drop and follow my friends out the door.

Ashlyn's heels clack against the cement walkway as she drags us past the line wrapping around the building and straight to the bouncer at the door.

*It's freezing out here, I'm not sure how Ashlyn is only in her silver dress with no jacket.*

The murderous glares from the people in line make me wish my sweater had a hood attached, so I could hide in it. The bouncer holds his hand up, ready to tell us where the back of the line is I'm sure, especially when he glances around Ash and takes in my yoga pants and over-sized sweater. I pull at the end kind of wishing I *had* changed. I shove those feelings down deep and dig out the fuck-it girl attitude that I'll be using as a shield all night.

That glance was the opening Ash needed. She turns his head gently back towards her using the tips of her fingers. His head tilts down to meet her eyes and ample chest that is barely contained in her silver mini dress.

Jaz and I watch as his gaze drifts to where her nipples pebble against the silk fabric as she whispers in his ear, saying who could fathom what. I see his eyes widen and turn glassy, his fist clenching. I look over at Jaz to give her the *Ashlyn is saying dirty things again look*, but she's already giggling at me.

Ash leans back, pulling the bouncer's attention as she waits. Slowly he nods and opens the door for us to the warmth of Club X.

We weave through the mess of people flooding the entryway leading to the wide-open dance floor with the bar at the back. I grab Ash's arm before we walk down the steps and into the main group of club-goers. "What the hell did you tell him?"

She smiles, leaning towards me. "That if he was a good boy and let us in tonight, he *might* get a reward when we're leaving."

I scrunch my eyebrows at her.

She tosses her head back and laughs, "We'll see what that reward will be. Maybe my number. Maybe I'll take him home later. I'll see how I'm feeling by the end of the night." She has a wicked look in her eyes when she grabs my hand and pulls me along. "Come on! Let's get a drink!"

I shake my head, letting her tug me through the crowd. I hook my other arm through Jaz's. With Ash parting the sea, we make it to the bar in record time. I plaster myself as close to the counter as I can, leaning away from the bodies pushing into me from all sides. My anxiety expands against my skin, I check the exits, ready to bolt.

*Why did I agree to come out tonight? I'm obviously not in the right headspace for this.*

Ash grabs my hand and sets a colorful drink in it effectively yanking me out of my panic. "What is it?" I yell over the music, the base thumping so loud it feels like my brain is rattling.

"Liquid cocaine! You'll love it!" Ash is in her element, forever the party girl. It's her coping mechanism for everything that happened to her. Jaz and I support her in any way she will let us, which isn't much right now. She needs to get through it on her own, but we will be here in the end. The same way I need to get through the disaster I've created for myself.

Ash drapes her arms over Jaz to get closer to her ear. "Let's start our project tomorrow! I have so many ideas..."

I tune them out as they start to discuss the remodel of the house they recently started on. Ash had extra money to burn and Jaz needed a new place to stay since she started her master's program. I guess if all else fails and I go broke, I'll just beg them to let me crash in their spare room. Or a pull-out couch. I can't afford to be picky at that point. I definitely don't want to have to go back to my mom's house. I visibly shake at the thought. *No thank you.*

I turn to take in the crowd. The wild dance floor with the gyrating bodies, sweat dripping on each other, oblivious to the frigid weather outside promising snowfall soon. I swirl my glass, searching for my straw and when it bumps into my mouth I suck down a good amount while my vision scans over to the VIP section.

*Fancy. Wow, Ash was right. This drink is amazing.*

The liquid sliding down is warming me from the inside making me feel cozy all around.

*I wish there was a chair I could curl up in, but it looks like they're all with the fancy people.*

I watch the group behind the fleece rope converse. The shortest man is having an absolute fit, yelling with his chest puffed up, hands flying in the air at the men seated before him in business suites. I chuckle to myself, sipping from my straw. "Wonder what crawled up his ass."

"We're going to dance!" Ash yells in my ear. My drink splashes on my sweater when I jump. I give her a thumbs up, trying to brush the liquid off my chest to no avail.

I'm in no mood to dance tonight. Well, for now. Who knows once the liquid starts flowing through my system.

Sighing, I go back to people watching. Ash drags Jaz onto the dancefloor, and they start seductively dancing together drawing the eyes of everyone around them. The VIP section has quieted down, but one of the seated men are missing. *Hmmm.*

I turn and scan the building. I'm invested. Turning to my right, I jump back when a man's face is inches from my own. My back slams into someone else, and I can't get away from the guy. He leers down at me from a couple inches above. His glazed eyes and slurred words tell me he's been here awhile.

I wave my hand at my ear and shrug trying to signal to him that I can't hear him, but it just encourages him to talk more.

"D'youuu have a d-d-date around 'ere?"

He leans closer to me. I try to get away but the bodies are pushing in from all sides, and I can feel my heart racing as the panic climbs.

# CHAPTER 4

## *James*

I MAKE my way to the VIP section after entering the crowded Club X. Ryder claims it would be the quietest part of the club, since the new client insisted on meeting us here. I argued that having it in a clean quiet office sounded like a better idea, but apparently, my old man mindset didn't get through, so here we are. There's nothing wrong with it I guess, I just don't have the patience for clubs and bars after everything that happened with my ex. This was the scene she lived for. Men chasing after her, trying to buy her drinks and take her home, even when she was already in a committed relationship. It didn't end well with the media trailing my every move and then hers, secrets tend to come out faster when there are cameras following everything you do.

A cocktail waitress stops me at the ropes and asks for my poison. If only she knew… "Whiskey is fine, thanks."

Apparently, the VIP section here only allows a

certain quality of liquor for the attendees to make everyone in here seem like more of a pompous asshole. This is going to be an expensive meeting, so this guy better sign our contract. This level of income will help us subsidize the smaller companies that don't have large marketing funds but could use our help. The smaller companies are the ones my dad always loved, so we are adamant about finding a way to make it work for as many as we can per year.

"JAMES! You made it." Ryder is screaming over the music and waving his arms at me from where he and the client sit on the couch. I already want to turn around and leave, but I guess I should give Thomas a little time to find something to eat before bothering him again. "James, this is Patrick. Patrick, this is James, the founder and CEO of Kemp."

I reach my hand out to shake Patrick's, but he slides it up his woman's shirt and grabs her breast, hard. She winces but leans into him. *Great.*

I shoot a look at Ryder, who grimaces but subtly rubs his fingers together in the telltale sign for cash. I slide my hand into my pocket, ready for this night to end. Alester walks up from behind me and pats my shoulder, then we both take a seat in the chairs across from Ryder and Patrick.

"What did you think of the packet we sent to your office regarding your future marketing opportunities?" I ask.

Patrick's other hand is resting on the woman's thigh

as it slowly slides higher. "You know, man, I haven't actually looked at it yet."

I look at Alester, and watch as his eyes narrow at the guy. "Are you ready to sign then? Or is this meeting a waste of our time?"

"Whoa, man. Let's just get to know each other for a bit before we start talking numbers," he says, and I want to punch him. I'm about to tell him we don't have time for this when he adds, "I'll make it worth your time. This will all be on the clock. Let's say fifty grand for the meeting? And if I like what I hear, I'll sign before I go home to Jessica here. Deal?"

I take in a long, slow breath, the mixed scents of booze and sweat threading through me. I need to calm down. "Deal. So, how do you two know each other?" I point to the woman in his lap.

His eyes light up. "I rented her for the weekend! It's crazy the things you can do with the level of money I have. She's an escort. I've never done it before, but there's a first time for everything."

I look to the woman. "Do you enjoy your line of work?"

"It's new, but yes, I suppose." Her words don't match the dead stare in her eyes.

I pull a business card out of my wallet. "I'm hiring quite a few positions, in case you want to change your career." She leans forward and takes the card from me. "We pay well, you could start tomorrow if you want, and you'd be working with a lot of other women. The number on the card will go to Stacy. You can tell her James gave you a card, and she can set you up. If that's something you want."

She slips the card into her small purse, water lining her eyes. "Thank you." She slides further away from Patrick, but he doesn't seem to care or notice. I watch his eyes dart around the club as he takes in a girl in a silver dress.

*Great. Is this just going to be us watching him chase women all night?*

I look around for the cocktail waitress with my drink, but I don't see her anywhere. It could be hours. After this little introduction I'm already checked out. "I'm going to the bar to get a drink."

"Get me one, man," the insolent child throws out, but I ignore him.

Pushing through the piles of bodies makes me more than ready to go home. Finally, the bar comes into view. I feel my mouth lift into a smile when I see a woman in a large sweater and spandex pants leaning against the bar. I'm jealous. I wish I could've changed into my sweats for this meeting. Then maybe we could avoid working with this guy altogether.

*No, the company could use the additional funds, so I need to suck it up. Every account matters. Technically we have plenty of money, as my net worth is now in the billions, but I like to gain more to donate to various charities, help smaller accounts, and invest in whatever new idea I can find.*

I continue to watch her, noticing now that she's trying to lean away from a man invading her space. Her head is swivels looking for a way out, but she's cornered. I grab a hundred-dollar bill from my wallet and hold it up for the bartender.

He drops what he's doing and jogs straight to me. Throwing his rag over his shoulder, he yells, "What can I get ya?"

"A double whiskey and a glass of red from your top shelf. Add it to the Edward tab. The cash is for you." I shout back then lean on the bar and wait as he grabs the bottles off the shelves.

I watch the skinny guy with tight pants put his hand on the woman's shoulder, which she pushes off immediately.

He yells towards her ear so loud that I can hear it across the bar. "Y-you lookin pretty cozy. Bet you'd l-look great draped across my couch!"

I can't see her face, but her head whips back and she glances at the ceiling.

*I've got to get over there.*

The bartender sets the drinks down, takes the money, and disappears. I pick up the glasses and make my way towards the two as he grabs her arm this time. I balance both drinks in one hand and shoulder-check the guy as I place myself between them. I don't spare a glance at the dipshit as I peer into the woman's wide brown eyes. "Sorry the wait was so long, baby. I got your wine."

She slowly sets down the green mixture in her left

hand as she takes the wine glass, glancing back and forth between me and the dipshit. "Thaaaanks...babe."

Her eyebrows draw together, but she quickly relaxes when she eyes my suit from bottom to top, then finally rests on my eyes. Whatever she sees must put her at ease. Her hand lifts to adjust her hair, but I capture it in my own, bringing it to my lips and leaving a light kiss. I don't know what's gotten into me or why I feel the need to protect this woman, but at this point it's the best thing that's happened to me all day, so I'm going with it.

Dipshit tries to shove my shoulder to get back at her, but I take my glass and dump the whiskey all over his front, causing him to cuss and jump back. I haven't taken my eyes off her, watching as the corner of her mouth lifts slightly, and I can't help but smirk back. The guy starts yelling something at me, but I'm not listening. Instead I bend towards her ear, "If you want a ride home, I have a car service waiting out front. Driver's name is Thomas. He will take you wherever you want to go."

I watch as she seems to think about it, then she leans towards me. "And what if I want to stay?" Her voice makes me want to throw her over my shoulder and go home. Fuck the meeting.

*What is wrong with me?* I think it's been too long since I've been with a woman.

I'm stunned for a moment, then I feel another shove on my shoulder, so I hold up a finger to the beautiful woman. I turn towards the smell of whiskey. The guy's face is bright red like a tomato, his fists balled and ready to swing.

I stand my ground. It's been a while since I've gotten in a fight, but I wouldn't mind some free stress relief.

Ryder ruins my fun and comes up behind Dipshit, placing his hand roughly on the guy's shoulder. The drunk idiot flinches and swings his balled hand towards Ryder.

Ryder catches his fist without even looking, a wicked smile stretching across his face as he looks down at the drunk. The idiot slowly lowers his arm when he realizes his eyes are at Ryder's chest and he has to crane his neck to see him properly.

"I think you're done here." Ryder's low tone promises violence if the man chooses to stay. Luckily, Dipshit shows some sense of self preservation and makes a run for the exit.

Ryder shrugs then glances between the woman and me. "Did you get Patty his drink?" When his eyes settle on me, I can tell this is going to end up being a bigger conversation later. *Can't wait.*

"No, and I'd rather not work with that idiot if possible."

The woman glances between us as we speak, slowly sipping the wine I handed her. I want to study every aspect of her, but unfortunately, I came here for business. Maybe she would wait for me.

Ryder throws his hands up in defeat. "I'll try to find another option this week, but he might be the best bet for this area. I'll keep him happy and entertained until we know for sure." He glances at her again with a curious look, but I make no move to introduce them since I have no idea what her name is. Ryder looks back and shrugs. "I'll grab the drinks and head back over there. We better start the discussion soon before Patty ends up too drunk to sign anything."

He makes his way to the bar holding out cash, and the bartender runs for him.

"Huh." The lanky brunette watches him.

I look at Ryder, trying to figure out what she sees when I ask, "What?"

She shrugs. "I had no idea I had to wave my money at him like a stripper to get him to give me a drink."

A laugh bubbles out of my mouth before I can stop it. "You hit up strip joints often then?"

Her lips turn up, and her eyes twinkle as she leans towards me, so I can hear her better. Her breath hits my ear, sending shivers down my spine. "Every night, well, except tonight obviously. I should have known better." She smirks and sips the wine.

I hope she's joking, but these days you never know. I gesture to her glass. "I hope red was the right choice. I couldn't see what you were currently drinking to judge."

"Red is great, actually." She glances at the other glass she left on the bar. "That was full of bad decisions and I've made enough of those lately."

I take in her words. "Sometimes bad decisions help us

feel alive." She runs her fingers across her lips, and I can't help but track the movement.

"Well, the night is young. Maybe I could make some more by the end."

Her eyes bore through me to my soul, lighting me up from the inside out. The pulsing need to give her the world aches through me, but that's not what everyone wants. I've learned that the hard way. But those deep brown eyes and long black lashes are making me forget...

# CHAPTER 5

## Alexandra

FLIRTING with this handsome man is helping me in ways I don't think he could ever fully understand. Hell, I'm not sure I do. I just know I don't feel guilty, and maybe that's a bigger sign that my short relationship with Taylor was never meant to last.

His phone buzzes in his breast pocket, and when we look over to the VIP area, his business partner is waving wildly at him. I watch his shoulders drop before he gives me a sad smile. "I should probably get to my meeting. Maybe I can see you after if you choose to stay? If not, Thomas, my driver, will be out front. I don't blame you if you decide to leave. I'd rather not be in Club X." He pauses and his eyes travel the length of me. "Well, meeting you has turned my experience around." He grazes his hand down my arm.

He looks back and groans, so I scan the area for Ash and Jaz, stopping dead when instead I see Taylor with the blonde. I reach out and grab suit guy's arm on instinct, setting my glass on the bar, all but forgotten. I look back at him, we lock eyes and fuck is it intense, but I need to focus.

"This might sound crazy," I say, "but I need your help for a few minutes to get me to my friends, then outside." He scrunches his eyebrows at me, probably unsure if I'm actually sane, so I quickly add, "My ex just walked in with the slut he cheated on me with a few hours ago. So, I'm very desperate to not have to deal with that alone right now and my friends are currently somewhere grinding on a bunch of guys or each other. Either way, they're too far away to help me right now."

I bite my lip, glancing from him to them. They're quickly approaching as he mulls over my request. "Here." I grab a napkin and pen from the bar, and quickly throw together a contract.

> *I, Alex, agree to provide one (nonsexual) favor sometime in the future pending you, Hot Suit Guy, assists in getting me away from ex- douche pants.*
> *X___________*
> *X___________*

I scribble a quick signature at the bottom and draw a line with an X for him to sign. I slide the napkin towards him quickly. "This might help since you seem like the type of guy who likes contracts...Please?"

He scans the note, smirks, then signs a name that is unreadable in the dim club lights, and slides it into his breast pocket. He looks over my head, and I watch as his eyes narrow, presumably on Taylor and his new side piece. "You have ten seconds before they reach us," he says. "What do you want to do?"

*Fuckkk*. I'm afraid to see how close they are now. My mind is spinning as I try to come up with something. At the sound of Taylor's high-pitch annoying laugh, I lock eyes with Hot Suit Guy. *How could I have ever been attracted to Taylor when men like this exist?*

Hot Suit Guy's eyes plead for an answer, but instead I reach up and grab his cheeks, dragging him down to me as I stand on my tip toes and crash my mouth into his.

Sweat trickles down my back as I worry that he won't kiss me back. It dissipates when I feel his hands slide to my ass and pick me up. I yelp against his mouth, but he keeps kissing me, sliding his tongue into my mouth. *Fuck, I didn't think it would go this far. I'm going to melt.*

The sound in my head goes quiet as his tongue turns my mind to goo. *Damn he's a good kisser. This was a great plan.* Heat travels across my body as I resist the urge to grind against him, very aware of how close his hands are to my center.

"Alexandra? What do you think you're doing?" Taylor yells from somewhere behind me, breaking the spell this man has on me.

Hot Suit Guy, *I really need to get his name, damn,* pulls back and I whine. *What the hell is wrong with me?*

His mouth pulls into a smirk. *Shit he heard me.*

I slide down his hard body as he slowly sets me back on the ground. I shiver, feeling every piece of him rub against me. Especially the bulge pressing into my belly. I guess I wasn't the only one having a good time. Fucking Taylor just keeps ruining my day.

"Hello?" Taylor draws out the word, working to get my attention.

I huff and spin around. "Can I help you?" My voice is laced with as much disdain as I can muster.

Taylor scoffs. "You really couldn't wait a day before hooking up with someone else?" He flings his arm towards the man next to me, which I find hilarious considering, well, everything. A laugh bubbles from my lips before I can stop it.

I feel Hot Suit Guy's hand slide across my back, wrap around my stomach, and pull me against him. "Let's go find your friends so we can get out of here. You don't owe him an answer."

I watch Taylor's eyes narrow as he glares over my head. He puffs up his chest, ready to respond, when the blonde next to him starts pouting and pulling on his shirt. He swats at her. Clearly he already forgot about the one he deemed worthy enough to ruin our relationship. His jealousy over someone he's never met and could never compete with is outrageous. I don't know why I never saw it before.

The man holding me takes that opening to glide us around Taylor, and I let myself get pulled towards the dance floor. He leans down. "What do your friends look like?"

"Umm..." Two bodies slam into me from either side, making an Alex sandwich.

"Oh my gosh! Are you okay?" Jaz asks.

"We saw Taylor!" Ash yells.

"And the kiss. We totally saw that kiss." Jaz pulls me close, setting a hand on each of my cheeks. "That was hot."

"Where did you find him? And so quickly." Ash adds.

"Guys!" I yell at them spinning my head towards Hot Suit Guy who is literally watching and listening to their entire performance.

"No, no," he says. "Don't stop because of me. I love this." He crosses his arms over his chest, and honestly, his muscles bulging under his dress shirt make me want to rip it off of him. Like now.

*Fuck. Me.*

"Oh—" Ashlyn starts, but I snap my fingers in her face, making her flinch.

"No." Her head snaps to me as she gives me puppy dog eyes again. "Nice try, but I'm going to get out of here."

"Uh no. 6-1-1! You can't. Under stipulation 4.2 you must stay at the designated destination no less than three hours." Jaz points at me, her eyes getting glassy. "Those are the rules."

*Dammit.* I look at Hot Suit Guy. "Name?"

He points to himself, a smirk still glued to his face. "James. Nice to meet you, Alex."

"Okay, James. It seems we have a problem. I can't leave for another two and half hours, and Taylor now thinks we're a couple." I glance over his shoulder at Taylor and grimace. "And he looks like he wants to kill me, sooo..."

"So, you need me to play along a bit longer?" He brushes a lock of hair behind my ear, and my body wants to melt. *What the hell.* "I have a meeting, but you can attend as long as you accept one condition."

"Is this your favor?" I ask.

"No, your contract is valid for the one interaction with Taylor. Now we are off script with an additional favor on each end." I huff but nod in agreement. I don't really have a choice. "Great. Our potential client is a prick, but the company could use him. So, as long as you don't do anything to make it go south, it shouldn't be a problem."

"Deal," I say. Then I look down at my sweater. This probably isn't the best attire for a meeting. I lock eyes with Jaz and she grins.

She strips off her jacket and hands it to Ashlyn. Then peels her black lace top off and holds it out to me. She puts her jacket back on over her leather bralette. I rip my sweater over my head leaving me standing in just a white lace bra. I grab the see-through top and slide it on.

Ashlyn's eyes bounce back and forth from Jaz and I. "Hot. Love it. Ditch the sweater." I raise my eyebrows. She knows I'm not made of money. "I'll buy you a new one for fucks sake."

I'm about to drop it when James takes it from my hands. "It's fine. It can come with us." His eyes rake over me with the same intensity as before.

*I guess he likes what's under the oversized sweater.*

He takes my hand, and we make our way towards the VIP section.

"Have fun!" Jaz yells.

"Do everything I would!" Ashlyn yells, laughing.

*God, I can't take her anywhere.*

When we pass the bouncer at the entrance a cocktail waitress runs over. "I can get you a new whiskey, unless you'd prefer something else." She waits with her hands gripped together like she's waiting for James to yell at her.

"A top-shelf bottle of red will be fine." He makes to walk us to his table, but she stops him again.

"That's ten thousand dollars. Are you sure?" Her voice squeaks at the end. Poor girl.

"Perfectly fine. Just add it to my tab. If that's all, we have a meeting to attend." He waits for her to take off for the bar before we move again.

"You didn't have to get the most expensive bottle." I say. I'm starting to feel like I'm way out of my depth here.

Especially wearing yoga pants. *Why didn't I make better choices?*

James squeezes my fingers. "The boss won't mind."

"Finally! You're back. We should get started," says the man who came over during the drunk idiot fiasco. He gives me a quick glance with a quirk of an eyebrow, but I see James shake his head out of the corner of my eye.

"Who—who's this lovely lady?" The short man slurs as he falls into the pretty woman next to him. She tries to slide away, but she doesn't have much room left before she hits the floor.

James sucks in an irritated breath, squeezing my hand slightly. "Patrick, this is Alex." He nods to each person sitting at the table. "Alex, this is Patrick, our potential client. Ryder you met at the bar." Ryder waves at me. "Alester is our tech wiz, and Jessica is a potential new hire."

Ryder leans in close. "Nice to meet you, Alex. What is it you do?"

My hands start to sweat. I try to pull free from James before he notices, but he grips me tighter, giving me a couple reassuring pulses. "She's not here for a job interview, unfortunately. Let's get down to business. We all have a busy night." James says as he slides two chairs together, then motions for me to sit next to him.

I zone out as they start talking about contracts and the background of Patrick's company. He seems like a rich slimeball. The cocktail waitress brings the bottle of red with enough glasses for the table. James fills one for me and leans close, grazing my fingers when he passes it to me.

I almost drop the damn thing when he refuses to break eye contact, my heart is racing like a teenager on a first date. What kind of voodoo is this man using on me?

"If I sign tonight, when can we have marketing up and running?" Patrick asks. He seems to be sobering up quickly. I glance at the contract lying in the middle of the table.

*The Edward Corporation agrees to handle marketing for Kemp Global at two and a half million for the first year agreeing to re-negotiate in the start of each fiscal year.*

I slap my hand over my mouth, my wine threatening to spew all over Patrick across from me. I hazardously gulp it down and start coughing like a raging idiot. That kind of money is life-changing, and every single person around this table is acting like he just said milk costs three dollars.

James reaches over, patting my back and rubbing circles. "Are you okay?"

"Yeah. I...just went down the wrong pipe." I cough a few more times before I get myself under control. I want to crawl inside my sweater that's draped across the back of James's seat with everyone at this table now watching me. *Kill me.*

James continues to watch me for a full minute, ensuring I am in fact okay before turning back to Patrick. "As long as payment is received, we will have a designer for this location hired and ready to start within this month."

"Two at the max." Ryder jumps in discreetly shooting daggers at James. "We recently secured the office space, but two should be more than sufficient."

Alester remains quiet, with his hands clasped in his lap.

They watch Patrick, waiting to see his next move. Patrick puffs up his chest, makes eye contact with me, then bends down, snapping the pen into his hand and scribbles his signature on the line. "I'll have the money wired tomorrow." He points to James. "Two months *max*, and I want to see this prestigious marketing everyone is talking about."

The look that passes over James's face can only be described as a lion cornering its prey. It would make me nervous if I hadn't been watching Patrick's horrendous behavior earlier.

"Perfect." James stands and holds his hand out for me while his other picks up my sweater. "Ryder and Alester will take good care of you tonight. Enjoy the club, on us."

I place my hand in his as I stand, never taking my eyes off of him.

"We have another event to go to," James says.

My eyebrows scrunch involuntarily, and James winks at me.

Patrick's obnoxious laugh echoes in the small VIP

area, "Perfect! You boys can learn something from me tonight."

I glance around the table as James leads me from this area. The look that crosses Alester's face as we abandon them is downright murderous. He doesn't seem like the type who wants to sit in Club X all night either. *Poor guy.*

James keeps ahold of my hand all the way through the club as we make our way out the front doors. The brisk pre-winter air whips through to my bones. I wrap my arms around myself, trying not to freeze.

James looks down. "Shit, here." He opens my sweater and slips it over my head. I quickly stuff my arms through the holes and curl in on myself.

James slides his suit jacket off and hangs it over my shoulders.

"You don't have to do that," I tell him. "I don't want you to be cold. I'll be fine." The warmth from his body heat is still attached to his jacket, and I never want to take it off.

"I love that you care, but I don't get cold easily." He tucks his jacket tightly closed and pulls me into his arms for added warmth. "Thomas is just around the block."

I feel his phone vibrate against my stomach. "Are you going to get that?" I ask.

He looks down at me, tucked in by his chin. Our lips are so close, and all I want to do is taste him again. "No need. I know who it is." His eyes dart back to my mouth, and I have a feeling he wants the same thing.

I push myself onto my tiptoes, stopping when my

mouth is hovering just before his. I can smell the lingering scent of whiskey on his breath.

I hear a door open somewhere behind me and a man calls out. "Sorry I'm late, sir. I was around the block when I got your text."

James's eyes never leave mine when he responds. "It's not a problem, Thomas. Eventually you'll have to give up the *sir*, though."

"Never, sir." Thomas chuckles.

James rubs his nose against mine slowly. "I guess we should get you in the warm vehicle."

I close my eyes, wanting to stay in this moment. "Come with me?"

He sighs, squeezing me closer. "Under one condition." I look into his eyes full of conflict. "I'll keep you company in the car and walk you to your door, but that's where our night ends."

Confusion mars my face, so he continues gently rubbing his hands up and down my arms. "This thing between us feels like it could be something, and..." He looks to the sky then back to me. "I'm over my one-night stand part of life." He watches me, but what the hell do I say to something like that? A man who doesn't want to just jump in my pants and leave. One who seems to have his life together when I'm an utter hot mess. No job and recently cheated on doesn't really scream wife material to someone like him.

Instead of saying something stupid, I keep my mouth shut and tug him towards the SUV.

Thomas holds the door open. I slide in and he shuts the door, then he makes his way around the SUV to open the door for James, who shakes his head. *What in the fuck is happening? What was in that drink Ash gave me?*

"Thomas refuses to let me get my own door, no matter how often I remind him that my arms work just fine," James laughs.

"I'm proud of what I do and how I do it," Thomas comments as he slides in the front seat and shifts the vehicle into Drive before pulling out onto the road. "Where to?"

"We will drop Alex off before going to my apartment." Thomas nods, but James turns to me. "Where do you live?"

I fidget with my hands. "Uh, Cambridge Apartments, by..."

"We know where they are. That's a nice location." James says. Thomas chuckles, and I feel my ears heat.

"What is it?" I ask, unsure if I really want to know why Thomas is laughing.

James takes in my change in demeanor. "Oh no. It really is a nice location. I just bought an apartment near there. I pass your apartment every day on the way to work. That's all." He places a hand on mine, and I feel my knee-jerk anger start to simmer.

"He's telling the truth, dear. I know exactly where your apartment is. Heck, I could probably drive there with my eyes closed. I won't, of course. That's dangerous." Thomas laughs to himself again.

I take a moment to look around the lush SUV with the fancy gadgets in the front and more in the back row. The leather feels like silk as I graze my hand across it. This is the most expensive vehicle I've ever been in. And the first with a driver! I feel like I'm in a dream, or a movie.

*This is all feeling very Pretty Woman.*

"How long have you been driving James around?" I lean forward, to meet Thomas's eyes in the mirror. I see James shake his head and laugh out of the corner of my eye.

Thomas lets out a deep chuckle that matches the pitch of his voice. "Years. We aren't from here. The company started in New York, but I go where the boys go. So, I moved over to Minnesota with James, Ryder, and Alester when the company wanted to grow. I know how it sounds, three boys from New York working at a company large enough to start a chapter wherever they please must be pretentious assholes. But they're great guys, they pay well, and they're basically family now."

James coughs and looks down, trying to stay out of the conversation. Thomas doesn't pay him any attention and continues. "They are all great with my little girls, and my wife loves to take them under her wing as her additional grown children. I obviously don't have boys myself, but if I did, I would hope they would act like them." I watch him smile to himself in the mirror.

"Come on now, even Ryder?" James jokes, nudging Thomas's shoulder slightly.

Thomas shakes his head at the thought, and I can't

help but laugh with them even though I've only just met Ryder. He definitely gives off the wild child vibes. But I obviously enjoy that, given that Ashlyn is my best friend.

"Yes, even that boy." He glances at James with a fond smile. "Ryder may be wild, but he's full of heart. And in a world like this, we can use all of the heart we can get."

I peek out my window. The amount of love in this car feels heavy compared to what I grew up with. I don't think either of my parents would ever be this proud of me, and here Thomas is, not even related but giving off proud dad vibes. I think about how my dad up and left us the second my sister turned eighteen. He wanted to travel the world without the weight of a family tying him down. We haven't spoken to him since.

Mom just throws herself at any event that comes up, trying to keep her mind off of the fact that Dad left, and wanting us to marry some rich man with ties to "high society," whatever that means. She grew up poor. The kind of poor where food was sometimes an unknown, and she doesn't want that for our futures. She takes *starving artist* in the literal sense. Maybe one day she will believe in me.

James places his hand on my thigh, bringing me back to the now, and I turn my head to meet his stare. "Where'd you go?"

I sigh. "No-where I'd like to go again." I rest my head on his shoulder. He lets my thigh go and makes soft swirls on my leg.

The SUV slows to a stop, and Thomas looks back at

us. "We have arrived. Would you like me to circle the block?"

I giggle. "That's not necessary. Thank you for the ride, Thomas. I've enjoyed your company."

James places a hand on his chest. "I'm hurt! What about my company?"

I shove him playfully. "I think it's pretty clear I've enjoyed your company too."

Thomas chuckles, opening his door then James's.

I reach for my door handle, but James pulls my hand into his. "Let me get it for you?"

"Okay," I whisper, his mouth close to mine. He steps out and walks around the SUV, speaking quietly to Thomas, so all I can hear is mumbled voices through the vehicle. Then my door is opening, and James is offering me his hand again.

"I don't think I've ever had a boy get my door and walk me to my apartment before," I tell him.

James tucks me in close to keep me warm on our short journey to my apartment building. "Like you said. You were with boys. Men take care of the women around them." He pulls open the door to my building and we start up the endless stairs. My cheeks are on fire despite the cold temperature outside.

Maybe he's right. Maybe I haven't been with a man.

I glance at him out of the corner of my eye. "Just how old are you?" I probably should have asked sooner, you know before he walked me to my apartment, but it never seemed like it mattered. Everything has felt so natural.

He smirks. "I'm twenty-eight."

I scoff. "Well, that isn't much older than me. You made it seem like everyone I've been with is an infant compared to you. I thought you were going to say mid-thirties or something."

We make it to my floor and I stop to look at him.

James places a hand on either side of me boxing me in as he looks down at me. "And what if I was mid-thirties? Would that scare you away?"

My stomach flips and heat spreads down. I have to fight hard to resist the urge to rub my legs together. I lift my head higher, taking in his green eyes flaked with gold as he holds my stare, waiting. "No. I didn't even know how old you were before I got in the car with you."

He tilts his head at me. "And what would make you run for the hills?"

I think for a moment and hum. "Probably if you were the type of man my mom tries to set me up with. Rich and pretentious. Flaunting wealth at every social event in the vicinity."

He laughs, unboxing me. "We'd better get you inside."

"Why?" I ask.

"Because if I stay in your orbit any longer, I'm definitely going to want more, and I don't think you're quite ready for that."

There goes my heart again. He backs down the hallway, never breaking eye contact.

"Wait! You forgot your jacket." I start to shrug it off but he holds up a hand.

"Keep it. It looks better on you anyway."

I slide my hands down the expensive jacket and can't help but smile.

James stops at the top of the stairs, waiting.

I smirk. "I'm safe. You can go home now."

He leans against the wall like he has all the time in the world. "I'll stay until you're safely tucked in your apartment with the door locked. I'll sleep better this way."

I shake my head and slowly open the door, slipping inside even though I'd rather stay in the hallway all night. My front door snicks shut and I lean against it, sighing. *What the hell just happened?*

I pull the pizza out of the oven as the timer continues to beep. "Ugh Shut up! Stupid thing."

I reach over, silencing it. I open every drawer in my small space looking for a pot holder, but can't seem to find one. *I just can't win lately.*

I grab a dishrag off the counter using it to grab the hot pizza pan. "FUCK!"

Throwing the sheet across the counter, I rush to the sink and throw cold water on my aching hand. I hiss as the water hits the growing red mark and rest my head on the cool metal ledge of the sink. "Why?"

I look over my shoulder at the offending pizza. It seems to have survived the throw only bouncing slightly on the pan. Pulling my hand out of the water, I take a good look at it. The redness has gone down slightly. It looks like I'll live to survive another attack from the world.

I slide my too-hot-to-eat pizza onto the chair I dragged next to the bathtub, with my large wine glass and glass of water. It's called balance. A sigh slips from my lips as I slide into the water and lean back.

My phone starts buzzing its way dangerously close to the edge of the tub, and I contemplate letting it fall for half a second before grabbing it.

"Hello?"

"Oh, honey. I was disappointed to hear you didn't get the promotion." I reach for my wine glass, rolling my eyes as I imagine mom pacing the kitchen, wondering how she is going to fix her problem daughter. "I'm sure you will prepare better for the next one." She pauses, "You are applying for another one, right?" I can feel the judgement seeping through the phone.

"I don't know, Mom. Right now, I'm just trying to

get through the day. I don't know what I want." I can't tell her I quit. She will freak out, and I'll never hear the end of it.

"Don't be so dramatic. That's no way to plan your future. You should be telling Taylor it's time to propose, so I can have grandchildren. I'm the only one in my friend group who doesn't have any!" Her voice goes up an octave, and I have to pull the phone away from my ear.

*Here we go again.* "Well Taylor is no longer in the picture, so there's no wedding in the future. You may have to look at Annabel for all future grandchildren." I take another drink and eye my pizza. "Look, Mom, I've got to go. I have an important work call coming in."

"You'd better explain about Tay..." Mom starts talking louder to get me to stay on the line, but I've had enough drama for one day.

"Sorry, have to go. Love you. Bye!"

I throw my phone into the hallway watching it ricochet. I wince, hoping I didn't just shatter it. "Shouldn't have answered. I know better."

I try to relax back into the tub, but all I can hear is mom and her comments. *Ugh.* Pulling the plug, I quickly towel off, put on sweats, and take my pizza into the kitchen.

I inspect my phone after I snatch it off the hallway floor. It looks to be in perfect condition. Bummer. I still don't have a new couch, so I plant my butt on a kitchen stool and pull open my computer search bar.

QUIET GETAWAY FOR ONE.

The first few listings that come up are less than ideal.

ROOM FOR RENT, SHARED BATHROOM.

"Who knows who lives there. Potential serial killer. No thank you." I take a large drink from my glass.

CONDO IN THE CITY

"No." I run my fingers through my hair then reach for a slice of pizza, scrolling with my other hand to the bottom of the listings. "Wait," I whisper like someone might take it from me.

SECLUDED CABIN IN THE WILDERNESS
EVERYTHING YOU NEED FOR A QUIET
WEEKEND TO DISCONNECT
NO WI-FI

*Perfect.*

Before I can put too much thought into it, I select a whole week, starting in two days, and type in my credit card information. It might not be the smartest decision I've made, given I just up and quit my job, but I've found that if I want to get anywhere with my art, I'm going to have to invest in myself. This getaway will be the perfect reset I need to dive back into what I want in life. The money will be a future me problem. I'll just have to bust my ass when I get back and apply for every job available in the marketing industry. All I need is someone to take a chance.

Finally closing my computer, I lean back with my pizza and smile.

I send a quick message to my sister, Annabel, expecting her to answer in the morning.

> Alexandra: Mom's on a warpath.
> Avoid calls for a while.

My phone immediately starts ringing for a video call, showing a photo of Annabel from our last vacation together. She's underwater with snorkel gear, her hand in a peace sign. We had both died laughing at it when we got to the room. It has been her photo ever since.

"Yessss." I plaster a smile on my face as my sister comes into view. Her blonde hair is piled on her head in a bun with makeup still on, but she has changed from her normal work clothing into a sweater.

"Dude. You could have sent that like two hours ago. I could not get her off the phone." Annabel rolls her green eyes. "What did she tell you because I have so much to fill you in on."

I slide further down in my stool, getting comfortable. "She just started on the usual... 'I need grandkids' blah blah blah. I cut her off and hung up the phone."

"Oh God. I can only imagine. I heard the same, but then she went on and on about you and your interview for a while. When she switched back to her drama with her friends, I just put her on speaker and let her talk. I think she's coming up here next weekend." Annabel raises her eyebrows at me.

"Don't look at me like that. I already booked a vacation. I'm getting out of here for at least a week. I need to take a much-needed break."

"What! Where? Can I come?" She laughs. Her blue eyes sparkle in the Christmas lights she already strung up all over her apartment.

"It's a secluded cabin in the woods up north with no Wi-Fi. I should probably check the weather, but it shows a nice big fireplace. I'm going to try to reconnect with myself and make a plan."

Annabel scrunches her face at the thought of being completely disconnected. She's more of a city girl with an all-the-amenities kind of vacation. That's probably why she chose to go to school in the largest city in our state. It's about an hour from where I live, so we don't hang out as much as we'd like. But video chats make it easier.

I pause wondering if I should tell her, but we tell each other everything, even when it sucks. "Don't tell Mom, but I kind of quit my job after the interview." I let out a breath I didn't realize I was holding.

Her eyes widen slightly before she chuckles. "Good! Thank God. It's time you got out of that shit-hole. It just wanted to bleed you dry by making you do three people's jobs and calling it preparation for future opportunities. I honestly can't believe you made it this long. I would have been gone the second they kept piling, who was the lady who left? Susie? Whatever her name was, her job onto my plate. Red flag, you know?"

I groan. "You're right. I just hate change and wanted to stay within my bubble to move up in life. But it clearly wasn't ever going to work out," I say as she smiles back at me from the camera.

"What are you going to do now?" She asks as she drags the camera into the bathroom and starts re-doing her makeup.

I run my fingers through my hair. I honestly have no fucking clue what I'm going to do, but I can't tell her that. So instead I tell her. "That's what I'm hoping this vacation will help me figure out. I want to try diving back into my art, but that's terrifying."

"You know what they say, life starts at the end of your comfort zone, or something like that." Annabel winks at me then goes back to applying heavy mascara.

I rub my eyes. "Yeah, I just need to make myself comfortable with being uncomfortable..."

"I think you can do it, and if you fail and run out of money, you can always sleep on our couch. I'm sure Jess won't mind!" She pops her big blue eyes open comically wide like she hopes I'll say yes, but she knows better.

Yikes, moving in with my younger sister and her roommate sounds like hell after living alone. Not that they're bad per se. Just that they're well in their party years and trying out the guy scene. Not to mention she's living an hour away from my friends and everything I love about my mini city life here. Whereas I'm happy to relax in my quiet apartment after a decent evening. Oh gosh, thinking about this evening reminds me of James. I am so not ready to tell Annabel about that whole encounter.

She doesn't miss a beat while I'm stuck in my head. "Well, Jess wants to go out tonight. Do you want to come? We will be leaving in a couple hours?"

"I actually just got back... so no. Plus I've been drinking, so I'm really not getting on the road and driving an hour to drink more." I grimace knowing the reaction that's coming.

"Wow, thanks for the invite." She pretends to pout but shrugs it off. Thank goodness. I can't deal with more family members being upset with me after everything. "It's ladies' night at some bar Jess found. She really wants me to meet someone, so why not? Sure you don't want to come back out? I'm sure I could talk one of Jess's guy friends to come get you." Annabel starts batting her eyelashes, and I can't help but laugh.

"No, no. You have fun. I've got to plan and pack and wallow." I look at my mess of food and dishes in the sink, sighing. "I should probably get on that. You should finish getting ready, unless you're going in sweats." *Like I did.* I look down at her shirt causing her to wince.

"You're right. Well thanks for the chat, I'll send you

the location of where we will be in case you change your mind. I love you."

"Love you, too." I end the call and put my phone on the charger to stay off of it for the rest of the night, choosing to bury myself in cleaning before I pass out for the night.

# CHAPTER 6
## James

THE NEXT MORNING, Ryder strolls into my office without knocking, again.

"Sure, come on in. I'm not busy." I continue typing up my email to Stacy, Ryder's assistant, who we brought with us for the expansion. She's handling setting up my interviews for next week, so we can get this location up and running. I'm hoping within three weeks we can start onboarding some of the staff and getting them settled into the flow. We pay a higher rate than our competitors because we actually realize how much work assistants do within the business. They keep everything running smoothly behind the scenes, especially when we are off doing other meetings. It's best to keep those people happy, thus the higher pay, bonuses, and holiday parties. We have noticed significantly less turn around with employees, which allows us to start new locations without the headache of additional new hires in our well-established areas.

Stacy has been getting raises regularly as we enlist her help with new locations. She's Ryder's top assistant, more like his second hand, really. They both make sure every other assistant has everything they need and keep up to date with new deals we make, as soon as we make them. He wouldn't be able to be his crazy self without her. Everyone has a role to keep everything running smoothly. Mine is more on the orderly side as Ryder and Alester have their own quirks to help us grow.

"Sooooo who was the girl who needed to take our ride home, thus making me find a cab in this new city?" He waves his hand around in dramatic Ryder fashion then leans over and hits the power button on my desktop screen, turning it black.

I look up. Ryder stands there in his dress pants and a T-shirt that says, Don't Follow Me Into The Darkness. I resist the urge to roll my eyes at him, barely. "Just someone in need of assistance. The cab wasn't that bad, you survived. What was bad was the douche boy you made me go out to the club for in the first place."

"No no no. We aren't changing the subject that fast. He could make us a lot of money. Hell, he already sent the deposit this morning which is helping fund everything here. His liquor company likes to spend a lot on marketing, and we could help him reach the New York market, which is making him ready to fork out even more than the contract states. Then we can focus on companies that need more assistance, like you like to do. You'll be fine. You'll survive a few awkward bar conversations." He plops into the chair on the other side of my desk, leans forward, and braces his chin in his hands and turns his brown eyes to me. "Who. Was. She. New prospect? Finally not going to be a lonely bachelor forever? Is she coming to the holiday party, the Fireside Ball, perhaps? Why was she in sweatpants?"

"No. No. No. They were yoga pants, not sweatpants. All I know is her name is Alexandra. Anything else?" I reach back and turn the monitor back on, so I can finish my email. I feel a ball hit my shoulder before Ryder stands again. I open my mouth to ask what his problem is, but he cuts me off.

"You're going to have to put yourself out there again sometime, James. Not everyone is like She Who Should Not Be Named. There are decent people in the world." He raps his knuckles on the doorway on the way out. "I'm here if you need me, man. Whether you like it or not." He smirks and dodges the ball I half-heartedly throw at his head.

He's not wrong. I probably should start dating again. Mostly so I don't have to eat alone every night. But the thought of letting anyone in the way I did with Rebecca and having it all come crashing down again makes me want to vomit. I really didn't realize how having money would change so many people around me. I never thought about having to worry if someone genuinely wanted to spend time with me, or if they just wanted to see how much money they could squeeze out before taking off. I never...

A knock on the door pulls me out of my spiraling thoughts. Alester walks in, dressed in his usual all-black attire. At least it's more fitting for work than Ryder ever looks, but we all just let each other do whatever we want as long as the work gets done.

He sets a cup in front of me and sips from his own. I take a drink. Black coffee, just what I need. I glance at him. "How's it going? Any issues I need to concern myself with?"

He drinks and thinks for a minute before sitting in the chair that Ryder vacated. "That client is going to be a problem, but I'll keep tabs on him."

This is news. "How so?" I ask, leaning back in my seat.

Alester sets the cup on my desk and folds his arms, making his muscles bulge across his black shirt. He's been hitting the gym more and more lately with the stress of opening another chapter and coming back to the midwest. I guess we are all handling it differently. I work more, Alester lifts weights, and Ryder takes a different woman to his bed each time. "The numbers are good, but the way he acted at the club after you left wasn't an image we want connected to our company. If he starts spouting that we are doing work for him, I'm concerned we will lose out on clients that suit our brand."

"What are you saying?" I wave my hands for him to get

to the point. "Just come out with it. It's just us. There's no HR here waiting to drag you into their office." I'm growing impatient. We need to set up this location and have it be successful, so I can possibly decide where to settle down in life. Our start up is doing so well in New York, but with everything that's happened these last few years, I really want to try to live my life like my dad was always telling me to. Maybe near my hometown, so I can try to go to the holiday dinners with Ryder and Alester again.

"Patrick is a dick. He was talking down to all the waitresses and grabbing some. I had to step in and rip his hand off of one, so she could leave the VIP area and do her job. He seems to think his money makes him entitled to do whatever he wants to whoever he wants. I won't sit back and watch that, and I don't want us being dragged down because of it. No amount of money is worth that behavior." Alester gives me a pointed look. "We both know what it's like to not have all of this. That man child doesn't seem to get that."

I rap my knuckles on the desk. Having grown up without money is the reason I make it a point to work with smaller or struggling companies. I give back to numerous lower-income companies, donate to charities, and own more properties than I know what to do with. I still have more than I need, but the company needs people like Patrick to fund the bigger projects. "Ryder seems to think that he's the only way to fund our larger side companies here," I tell Alester. "There's quite a few

I'd like to get on our books, and partnering with Kemp can make that happen."

Alester scoffs. "Then Ryder needs to go hunting for more rich assholes because I can tell you now, this is going to be an issue."

"Okay." I pull up a new email to Stacy to outline a new limited contract. "You're the tech guy. Find dirt that we can use to keep Kemp in line, and track his money and location. If he steps out of line, we will end it. I'll draft a new contract limiting our work and outlining additional amendments to what we allow in his personal life and how we want our company branded by him. If he goes against any of the terms, we will terminate his contract and make a public statement stating why and what kind of companies we stand with." Alester sips from his cup, his black hair swooping into his blue eyes as he nods. "Best case, he cleans up his act and we don't have to make changes. Worst case, we have to make a couple speeches at the Fireside Ball in a few weeks. I'll add an amendment that we still keep the deposit and half the year's agreement. Maybe then he will listen. If not, at least we will have a good amount to fund employees and a couple smaller projects."

He coughs. "You mean, you will have to make speeches. You know Ryder and I don't do those. That's why you have the bigger share, boss."

"Ugh. I hate when you call me that." I grab another ball from the basket and launch it at him, but he catches it easily. "We came up with this company together, remember?"

"Yeah, yeah, but it was mostly you. We just offered our expertise in other areas. Plus, your dad is the real bread winner here. Sorry, was. How are you doing with everything?" Alester asks. If it was anyone else, I don't think I could give a real answer. I'm just pre-conditioned to give the 'fine' response.

I take a deep breath and let it out slowly. "I honestly don't know. Sometimes I forget he's gone, and I pick up my phone to call him only to realize I can't anymore. I'm trying to do more things to make him proud, but it's hard."

Alester gives me a knowing look. "You're free to take time for yourself whenever you choose. I know it's been years, but that doesn't make it easier. Ryder and I can pick up the slack and set up this area. We all know Stacy is the one handling most of the candidate information at this point. We just have to fully vet them in person. But I get it. It's your baby. We're here for you in whatever capacity you need, man."

I nod at him as he gets up, heading for the door. Alester and Ryder are basically my brothers, we've been together our whole lives, our moms being the kind of sisters that loved being in each other's business every single day. It was basically like we had three moms we could go to for whatever we needed. Now we have two, but it doesn't feel the same for me. We wouldn't have it any other way, even if we bicker at times. They're family and now that Dad is gone, they're all I have left. I should get a cat or a German Shepherd or something. Someone to keep me company at home.

Alester gives me a two-finger salute as he heads into the hall. "Let me know if you need anything, or when we are ready to vet candidates."

Without looking back, he goes down the hall to his office full of computers where he keeps track of all of our IT issues, spreadsheets, and background checks that go beyond the regular limits. It's how we keep the best of the best for staff and how we know what they need from us to stay the most competitive. Is it fully ethical? Maybe not, but it ensures we have happy employees who don't drown in debt, but they aren't aware of this little tidbit.

Ryder, Alester, and I may operate differently within our company, but we have to keep the boat steady and reduce waste in training, and it helps us retain a higher income overall. We decided higher spending in the forefront to invest in the best employee was worth the risk. Alester keeps our cost analysis sheets up-to-date, so we continue to run smoothly.

I shake off my rabbit hole and jump back into reviewing the applicants that Stacy deemed worthy of our time. The less resumes I have to go over the better. I pick my top choices for a few positions and shoot them over to Alester to do a deep dive for the best out of those choices.

After a few more hours, I close my programs and lock down my office before heading home for the night.

# CHAPTER 7
## *Alexandra*

THE PHONE KEEPS RINGING, and just as I think it's going to go to voicemail, she answers. "Whh-hyyyyy the hell are you calling this early?" Ashlyn's groggy voice comes through the line, and I hear her bedsheets rustle as she burrows deeper into her bed.

"Seriously? It's 10a.m. Why are you still asleep?" I've been up since 6a.m. pacing and trying to figure out what the hell I'm going to do. Mostly spiraling and not getting much done, but I couldn't sleep, so here we are.

"Ugh. Okay, Mom." I laugh as Ash huffs and stomps across her room. "Obviously I met a *friend,* as you say, and things progressed rather late last night." I hear running water echo through the phone.

"The bouncer? So, you're not going to work today, then?" I walk over to the bar-stool and sit as I listen to her move around her apartment.

"Maybe. Oh that. I'm sick. Cough, cough."

I hear a loud thump then cussing across the line and try to hold in my laugh. "You can't say 'cough' when you're faking it. Please tell me you didn't do that when you called in?"

Ash scoffs. "Obviously I sent an email. I'm not dumb. Although I probably shouldn't read said email." I hear the distinct snap of a pod being secured in her coffee maker.

"Whyyyy?" I drag out the word, but internally I'm already laughing at her ridiculous behavior. *Never change, bestie.*

"Because I sent it when I was still slightly intoxicated. Who knows what I put in there?"

I can't contain my laughter and hearing her groan just makes it worse. I try to catch my breath as she yells at me to pull it together.

"You're insane. Want to go couch shopping?" I ask, already knowing the answer.

"Obvi. Let me get ready. I'll tell Jaz she's sick too. Cough, cough."

I laugh, shaking my head as she refuses to actually cough.

"Be there in an hour," she says before hanging up.

I quickly grab my purse and head down to the coffee shop a block away. I have coffee here, but it just tastes better when someone else makes it for me. I grab one for Ash and Jaz along with pastries because we can't go shopping on an empty stomach. That's ridiculous. I hustle back to my apartment after escaping the crowd of people fighting over a table in the tiny cafe.

With the coffee and pastries delicately balanced on the drink tray, I slowly make my way up the steps, careful not to splash hot liquid across my white jacket. I'm breathing heavily by the time I reach my landing. I should really get to the gym more, or at least get some cardio done. I've lived in this building for years, you'd think I'd be used to the stairs by now, but no, I'm over here wheezing like my lungs are barely functioning.

I balance the drinks in one hand and try to reach my keys inside my purse with the other. "Shit, shit, shit." I mutter and throw my purse on the ground to catch the leaning drinks at risk of causing third-degree burns to my chest. A bead of sweat forms on my brow from the anxiety of almost burning myself. I look down at my bag upside down on the hallway floor. "Shit."

I gently set our bounty on the floor while I flip my bag over, effectively spilling the contents everywhere. *Why me?*

I pluck my keys out of the mess and toss them towards the drinks before trying to collect everything else. I crawl to the scattered lip gloss rolling across the uneven concrete. "Gotcha!"

"Jesus," I hear someone whisper behind me.

I close my eyes against the heat crawling up my neck. *Jesus indeed. Every damn time.*

I slowly straighten, grabbing my keys to unlock my

door, and letting the rest of my mess stay where it lays. I try to avoid the man behind me, but he speaks again. "Let me get that for you." I hear dress shoes snap across the floor coming closer. I'm painfully aware of the fact that I'm currently in yoga pants, an old T-shirt, and a light jacket that I felt would be good enough to run down to the coffee shop, but it's definitely nowhere near the level of dress shoes behind me.

"That's fine. I've got it." I throw my door open and turn, ready to grab my stuff that's still strewn everywhere, but as I turn he's handing me the drink tray. My eyes snap up to his as I reach for it and pause. "It's you." I pause. *Great. Just what I need.* Fucking Clay is holding my coffee order. I narrow my eyes at him, giving him my best fuck-off face. "Are you stalking me?"

He gives me a slimy smirk that makes me want to slap it right off his face. "You wish. I actually just moved in across the hall."

I snatch the drinks from him and set them on the entryway table so I can pick up the rest of my purse lying all over the hall. "Good for you."

He stands against the wall, watching as I throw things back into my bag as quickly as possible. "Aren't you excited to see me? You know, since you can't see me at work anymore. I guess we won't have to worry about HR whenever we decide to have a late night get-together."

I gag loud enough he can hear me, but he just smiles like I'm kidding. I toss my purse over my shoulder, finally getting everything I threw out like an idiot. "Well, this has been fun, but you will never hear from me. Especially late at night. Have a great life, and enjoy the promotion." *Why in the fuck isn't he at work?* "Obviously you haven't started yet, or you just don't care."

"Tsk, tsk, Alexandra. You know they don't care what I do. A long lunch, leave early. It's all about the connections. One day you'll get that." He laughs, and I feel my anger about to explode.

"Cool." I slam the door in his face, so I don't say something stupid. I'm so irritated by him that I don't hear the clacking of stilettos down my hallway until Ashlyn is walking through my door and waving a hand in front of my face.

"We are ready to shop! Oh! Coffee, yum." Ash rushes over and takes a big drink before digging through the pastry bag, with Jaz following quickly behind.

"Wait. Why do you have your backpack?" I ask Jaz, who looks like she's about to fall over with how much her leather bag is bulging behind her.

She finally slides it off her shoulder, and it slams to the ground. I'm surprised it didn't break my floor. "Oh, well, I was in-between classes when Ash said we were playing hooky and going shopping, so I figured I'd just bring it in case there's down time."

"No no no. No studying allowed on hooky day," Ash mumbles over a muffin.

Jaz's face reddens. "The semester is almost over. Then you'll have me all winter break." She pauses. "Well, at least whenever I'm not working. I got a job with the

Department of Natural Resources for the winter as a trial, then hopefully they hire me full time."

I grab my coffee off the tray. "Awe. Our little tree hugger. We are so proud of you. You'll get the job, no question. Once they see how amazing you are they won't want to lose you." She looks down, picking up a pastry and avoiding our supportive faces.

Ashlyn claps, "Alright, until then...Let's go burn some cash and find an awesome couch that you can christen tonight."

"Ash! We aren't going out tonight. There will be no christening of any kind." I swipe my purse off the counter as we make our way out. Once they follow me into the hallway with the drinks and treats I lock up the apartment.

"That's what you think," Ashlyn says over the clacking of her heels down the long hallway. I'm not quite sure why she wants to go up and down all my stairs in those treacherous things, she's lucky the snow hasn't fallen yet.

I shake my head. Jaz loops her arm through mine as we follow behind Ash.

After hours of shopping and stopping for lunch, we stand on the sidewalk and watch as the delivery guys work to set my new couch on the grass because I didn't pay extra for them to deliver it inside the room. How was I supposed to know that meant only to the curb?

"Al, no offense, but how are we supposed to get this upstairs to your place?"

"Yeah," Jaz points at Ash's pink stilettos. "Especially with those."

"We can do it. We are strong, capable women." I hold my conviction as I watch the men struggle between the two of them before dropping it with a loud thud.

Jaz and Ashlyn share a look. "I'm all here for powerful women, but part of that is admitting when you need help."

I crouch down in the grass, staring at my new couch, willing an idea into my head. *How in the fu…*

The slam of a door jars my thoughts. "Do you ladies need some help?" The timber of James's voice vibrates all the way down to my lady bits. *I definitely don't need to be doing that anytime soon.*

"Yes." "No." Jaz and I say at the same time. I glare at her, she smiles back.

"Don't listen to her. She's too stubborn for her own good," Jaz states as she starts explaining the reason the couch is not already inside of my stupid apartment. I look behind James as Thomas steps from the front seat of the black SUV.

"Hey, Thomas. We can figure it out, honestly," I say as he makes his way over to me.

He chuckles, giving me that look fathers give their stubborn daughters. "You know he won't let that happen. He doesn't have it in him to walk away from someone in need." His eyes sparkle. "Especially you."

*What does he mean, 'me'? What do I have to do with that equation?* I don't get a chance to ask because James turns to me and my brain all but shuts off.

"Let me make a call and we can have this in your living room in twenty minutes." He steps off to make the call and I turn to my friends.

"What are you doing?" I whisper yell with my eyebrows raised damn near to my hairline. Thomas snickers behind me, but I pretend he's not there. He has daughters, so he will be exposed to this soon enough.

Ash wiggles her eyebrows. "That's the hot guy from Club X isn't it?"

"That's him? Damn, I approve." Jaz is outright ogling his ass as he talks on the phone. I groan into my hands.

"Oh my god. Kill me now. Could you keep your

voice down?" I whisper and glance over my shoulder seeing him strolling back. I shoot a look to Thomas and he gestures zipping his mouth shut with humor dancing in his eyes. Yeah, he's enjoying this.

"They'll be here in two minutes." James tucks his thumbs into his pockets like he has all the time in the world to help random females move couches.

"Who's 'they'?" I grimace at how bitchy that sounded. Taylor left a mark and it's still bleeding internally, I guess. "Sorry, thank you. I'm just having a week."

He smiles, and the way the gold flakes in his eyes are glinting in the late afternoon sun is not helping my insides at the moment. It's like whiplash knowing I just got cheated on, but my insides are smitten with the idea of someone new.

"Don't worry about it. My cousins are close by and willing to help. The guys you met at the club the other night." He shrugs like it isn't a big deal, but it definitely feels like a big deal.

"Ah, yes. I remember them." I just hope they aren't grumpy about helping me today, since they didn't seem very happy during that meeting.

Just as Ash is about to jump in and ask him a million questions about God knows what, another black SUV pulls up to the curb next to my new couch wrapped in plastic. I keep trying to sneak glances at James, but every time I look over, we make eye contact, and I quickly look away. He's not making this easy on me.

"Your knights are here, my ladies. We take payment

in beer and lap dances," Ryder says, his lips pulling into a smile as he runs his fingers through already disheveled blonde hair. The slightly taller dark-haired cousin, Alester, throws his elbow into Ryder's stomach making him cough. "I'm just kidding of course. Don't mind him...we don't. Nice couch, where do you need it?"

I rub my temples, but before I can answer, Ashlyn is stepping closer to Ryder. "First, what are your names? You know, in case you all are actually insane and I need to file a report later? Second, lap dances can be negotiated after a job well done." She's down-right purring as she rakes her eyes over him.

"Ashlyn!" *God I'm never getting out of this alive.* "It's the third floor. Thank you for your help, don't listen to that one." My face is burning and I'm sure the redness is really stark against my pale skin.

"Oh, I don't know about that. I think listening to Ashlyn is my new favorite hobby." His eyes practically sparkle. "I'm Ryder, and this tall drink of water is Alester." Ryder smacks Alester on the back, but he doesn't budge.

"We met at the club, but I'm Alex." I gesture to Jaz by the couch. "This is Jaz, and you unfortunately ran full force into Ashlyn. I obviously made a grave error in not accepting the full delivery charges."

James steps up to the end of the couch, nodding for his cousins to move into formation. "Not a problem, we're happy to help." His shirt is straining to hold the bulk of his arms in. That poor dress shirt. I definitely shouldn't have let them help with each of them in suits.

"Yeah. I can add more to my workout regimen. This won't be an issue." Ryder slightly flexes through his button-up shirt that's already hugging his arms. Alester grunts, swatting Ryder in the chest, before going to the other end and lifting the couch like it's a feather. With James on the other end, also having no issues with my cheap new couch, Ryder ends up being the coordinator and comedian, yelling out directions through the stair-well and up through the door to my apartment.

Once it's placed, Ryder starts to unwrap the plastic, ignoring me when I tell him it's not necessary. "This is a nice couch. Why'd you get a new one? Did you never have a couch? I should probably get a new one for my place…" Ryder yammers on without taking a breath.

"Once you get a place, you mean?" Alester raises an eyebrow at Ryder who shrugs and jumps on the freshly uncovered couch, making himself comfortable.

"She found her ex fucking some chick on the last one, so we obviously had to burn it, figuratively of course, and go shopping." Ash lets out as she's looking through which snacks she wants to eat next, then stop-ping the search when she realizes what she just did.

"Ugh." I wish I could bash my head into a wall right now.

Ash mouths 'oops' at me, while Jaz shakes her head. I can feel James's eyes on me, but thankfully he doesn't say anything, I'm sure he remembers the club incident.

"Yeah, that seems like a good reason to have a new couch. Too bad you couldn't have done something to him, but I guess there's always later," Ryder says with his eyes closed like he's going to take a nap. Alester grunts his approval and moves to sit on the couch, throwing Ryder's feet off of it to make room.

"Is he always like this?" I turn to James fully, and he laughs. The deep rich sound surrounding me like a cocoon and sending tingles to areas that should be ignored until further notice. They obviously can't be trusted after Taylor.

James's eyes light up, and he reaches a hand towards me. "Actually, I want-..."

"Oh! Our meeting!" Ryder runs a hand through his hair and bounces to the door. "We have to go, like now, this client was impossible to get a sit-down with."

"Wait a minute." Ashlyn stops him in his tracks. "You all work together? And you're cousins...Is this a joke? You look nothing alike." She's not wrong, but I also wasn't going to question the guys that just helped move that heavy ass couch like it was nothing.

"Uhhh..." Ryder looks to Alester, who shrugs, then to James.

"Our moms are sisters, but our dads' genetics obviously took over." I watch as James mulls over what he's going to say next, running a hand through his hair. "We started working together in college and never stopped." He shrugs. "We mostly like working together. Ryder gets a bit obnoxious."

"Hey!" Ryder yells and tries to dive for James, but Alester grabs him easily.

"Joking, joking. Kind of." James turns to Ashlyn. "Not a huge deal, just family business."

She looks unconvinced, but if they had grown up with parents like Ashlyn's they'd understand why she doesn't get the whole hanging out with and working with family. Still, she doesn't say anything or voice why she doesn't get it, so I keep my mouth shut too.

"I'll go start the car, so we can get to the meeting," Alester says and looks towards Jaz one more time before heading out the door with Ryder on his heels.

James turns to me, a slight brush of his fingertips on my arm. "Uh, I guess I'll see you around, sorry. I wish I could stay and talk to you more, but this really is important."

I struggle to suck in air, wishing my body would turn to stone and stop trying to lean into this man's touch. "That's okay. Thanks for your help again. We really wouldn't have been able to handle moving that monstrosity as much as I wish we could." I awkwardly wave my hand and instantly regret it. *Why am I like this?* "Thanks again...Have a good meeting."

James smirks at me as he walks backward out the door. "See you around, Alex."

My face is in flames as he closes the door. After watching James's arm porn while he carried and gently placed the couch, I think I need a cold shower. I'm afraid to ask the girls if they were also that aroused, or if it's just me and my newly single mind.

"Holy shit! I think my ovaries just sang to me!" Ashlyn says not a moment after the door shuts behind them.

Jaz shushes her. "What if they hear you!"

"Oh! You like one too? Good. Maybe they'll come back if they hear me!" Ash yells louder at the door, ready to run over and whip it open at a moment's notice. I have a feeling the guys are long gone with how long their strides are.

I laugh, watching them go back and forth, making my way to my new couch. I plop down on the cushion; it doesn't have as much bounce as my old one because I didn't have the funds to splurge on another expensive piece. Especially given that I just quit my job. I've been saving a lot over the years I've been working, so money won't be an urgent issue for a little bit, but I definitely need to find a job soon. I run my hand over the rough fabric and smile.

"What are you smiling about?" Jaz sits next to me, bouncing up and down, testing the seat.

I sigh, leaning back. "Just happy I don't have to look at the other couch and think about how shitty Taylor is."

"Yes, he's trash. There's much hotter fish in the pond...like James." Ashlyn arches her perfectly sculpted brow at me as she crosses her arms.

I scrunch my nose at her. "I don't think that's..."

"Shit!" Jaz jumps off the couch. "I forgot I have class. Ashlyn, can you drop me at campus?"

Ash grabs her purse. "Ah yes, your chauffeur awaits. Enjoy the new couch, and maybe break it in sometime." She winks at me as they run out the door.

I really wonder how James and his cousins got into the work they're doing. Honestly, what the hell do they do that they were in Club X for a business meeting? Especially for a company like Edward Corp. It doesn't make any sense. I shake my head. Not my business. I try to focus back on myself. I need to figure out my next steps. *What am I going to do for work?*

If it was up to Mom, I'd just find a man to take care of me and start a family, but that's not what I want. Not right now, anyway. I want a purpose and I need income. I've always dreamed of selling my art, but my parents were always quick to tell me to be practical.

Practical isn't making me happy. I need to take a risk. I guess quitting on the spot wasn't a great idea. *Ugh.*

I need to get out, clear my head, dive into my art, and see if that's something I can do. I'm going to need examples if I'm going to find companies to pitch myself to.

*Time to get my life together.*

*Shit.*

IT'S the morning of my trip and I'm buzzing with excitement to finally get away and paint. My front door rattles before I hear the tell-tale clacking of stilettos on my floor. "Hellloooo! We're here to help you pack and drink before you head out on your big vacation without us."

I glance up at Ashlyn as she strolls through the door carrying an oversized insulated bag that looks like it weighs more than she does. I shake my head, laughing. "I already told you this is a me trip. I need to get out of my head and figure out what I want to do with my life, my next steps. Also, who wears heels in the snow?"

"I think we know what your next step is. Wine. And for your information, I will never ruin an outfit just because the weather doesn't want to agree to be sunny all year round." Ash hefts the bag onto my little breakfast table, Jaz stabilizing it before it can slam to the floor.

"Plus, the first snow isn't until later tonight when I will be tucked securely in someone else's bed."

I try not to roll my eyes at her. "You know what I mean, but yes, wine is good. Especially now that we have a nice clean couch to hang out on."

"Ahh, yes. I was wondering if we were going to discuss the hot men that helped move this great new couch." Jaz rubs her hands together dramatically. "I call dibs on tall, dark, and mysterious."

"Seriously? How can you already know which one you want? They're all so edible." Ash inspects her perfectly manicured nails. "I thought we'd all take a turn then discuss the best option."

"Ashlyn!" I smack her arm as she tries to bat me away.

"What? I'm not shy. They're all hot, what can I say? But I guess Jaz can have first dibs. It's fine." She pretends to pout as Jaz launches a pillow at her face.

"Back off. You have your run of the town, no judgment. But you know maybe I could try to make a connection." Jaz looks down and starts pulling out the numerous snacks Ash brought within the bag.

Ashlyn and I share a glance, hearing the seriousness seep into the conversation. "Whenever and whatever you're ready for, we are here to support you." I slide next to her and snuggle my head into her shoulder.

Ash comes to her other side, doing the same. "Yes, I'm a great wing woman. I'll have things all lined up in no time!"

Jaz whips her head towards Ash so fast I have to

dodge out of the way to avoid a collision. "No no no no. I'll do it myself. Just throwing out my claim for a possibility."

"Alright, deal. Let's take some snacks to the bedroom, so we can get this party started." Ash grabs the bag of chips and a bottle of wine before walking down the hall. I quickly get glasses from my cabinet to reduce the risk of her spilling it all over my carpet. Jaz takes peppermint chocolates out of the bag and follows us.

By the time I round the corner, my suitcase is full. "Uh, what did you throw in there? Everything?" I ask.

Ash closes the drawer to my workout clothes quickly, "No." She drags the word out. "You won't be exercising, so you don't need that."

I pick through some of the items in the large suitcase. "Ash, this is all lingerie and short shorts...in the winter. What do you think is going to happen on my trip?"

She huffs as Jaz giggles, quietly eating the chocolate, her eyes darting back and forth like Ash and I are in a sparring match. "Look, I just think you need to dive back into your sexuality while you're away on your solo trip. And if you happen to take some sexy nudes while in a cabin in the woods, well then all the better for when you're back and on the market."

I stare into her blue eyes, my resolve breaking as I clutch the lingerie harder before throwing it back into the bag. "Fine. Fuck."

I haven't worn these sets since I first bought them and Taylor acted like they were a bigger inconvenience than anything. I guess I know why he didn't care now, too busy with work or sleeping with other women. Who knows how many. I had stuffed them into the back of my drawer ready to never see them again. Ash is right, I should just wear them for me. Maybe it will help me get out of my head with my art and really embrace myself all around. Sounds terrifying.

I look through the rest of the bag and sigh. "Really? Not one pair of sweatpants? Why?"

She blinks at me. "Why the hell would you need those? You showed me the photos. Cozy fireplace, cozy cabin. You'll be fine, just add more wood to the fire and it'll keep you warm enough." She grabs some sleep shirts from my drawer and throws them in. "There, clothing. Now you can go braless. Free the boobies."

Jaz chuckles. "Alright. Are we done packing then?"

"Ugh, just let me get my hair and makeup things then we can be done." I hustle to the bathroom and toss everything into my bag along with my art supplies.

"I'm starving, I'll find something to whip up for us." Ash runs for the fridge before I can stop her, "Uh, babe. What the hell is this?" I hear her yell from the kitchen.

I bury my face in my hands. "I haven't had time!" I holler back and peek around the corner. "Just eat the snacks you brought. It'll be fine!"

"What?" Jaz pops out of my bedroom. "It's empty again?"

Ash yells back. "Yeah. We need an intervention. Alright, let's go down the road and get brick stone pizza!

I can't survive on just chips and chocolate." Her enthusiasm is contagious as we all slip on our shoes and run out the door laughing.

I'm so lucky to have these two amazing women in my life. I'm not sure where I would be without them.

SITTING AT MY DESK, I can't seem to get a certain brown-haired woman out of my head as I glance at my calendar. I really need to get my shit together and ask her out, especially now that I know she only lives a couple blocks away from my apartment. I make a mental note to have Alester look into her, find anything that might be alarming. I can't have another Rebecca on my hands, the media would eat me alive, and I'm not sure if I can handle going through it again. It's best if Alex doesn't know the entire extent of what I do for a living.

I almost jump as Ryder comes barreling through the door, too buried in my own thoughts. "What are you still doing in here?" he asks.

"Come on in, again. I'm checking my emails and calendar for the day. Is something on fire?"

He blinks at me and taps the doorway. "Well, you're ten minutes late to our interviews already, so I'd say something is definitely happening." His eyes light up. "Oh! Is it that girl...what's her name again? Did you ask her out? Where are you going? Are you texting? Am I in the wedding?"

"Jesus. Calm down. I don't even have her number yet." I scrub a hand over my face. It's not like me to forget meetings, but I have been a tad distracted lately. I look at Ryder who's watching me as if I grew another head. "Well, let's go then. Don't want to keep...whoever they are...waiting. We need to fill these vacancies." I grab my tablet and make my way around the desk. Ryder tries to block the doorway, but I reach out and shove him onto the couch.

"Hey! Maybe if you stop going to the gym so much you wouldn't be able to take me." He launches back off the couch, gearing up to tackle me, but I sidestep him at the last second. He has to pivot to avoid slamming into the doorframe.

I pinch my eyebrows together. "And why would that be appealing to me? Why don't you just spend some time bulking up a little?" Ryder isn't small, just a few inches shorter than me and has more of a lean muscle instead of extra strength training.

"Hmmm." He takes off to the conference room where Alester is waiting for us to start prepping before the endless interviews start for the day. I despise interviews, but they need to be completed, and we are all on the same page about finding the right person for each role. We are looking to expand assistant positions, paralegals, IT, and we need to figure out which companies we want for janitorial and security. We may hire the last two in-house, but it's always good to have options. We look at what they've accomplished but we also dig deeper and like to get a feel for their personality. It's not a traditional interview, which throws most people, but the right candidate enjoys it.

"You made it," Alester says. "We have a full day, so we should probably start looking at which roles we will want to fill in the next couple of days or weeks. First, we have more assistants to interview, since they're the backbone and help the most behind the scenes. We need at least three more to start I would think, then we can circle back and look for more. We have ten interviews to get through today for them, so if we like more we can keep them." I nod, having already read our plan the night before, but Ryder is rapidly taking notes.

I shake my head at Alester, who smiles before continuing.

"We need a designer-slash-marketing person for our campaigns. We can start brainstorming what posting we want to make for it, or if we want to hunt online ourselves, keep your eyes open for artists that you find interesting. We can talk to legal if we need another person here or just relocate someone from our other branch to cover policies here. Maybe a few scouts for companies or generic job duty that we can send to shmoose when we aren't available." Alester flips rapidly through his notes, trying to quickly cover every barely relevant position, there will be more later when we are more functioning here.

He throws his finger in the air. "Oh! And we have a few IT slots we are interviewing today, almost forgot. Otherwise, this branch will stay pretty small with mostly us and people to assist, until we find the new leadership for this location, *if* we plan to move back to New York." His eyes lock onto mine in silent communication. He doesn't know if I'm staying here. We briefly talked about the possibility to be closer to our family, but it wasn't a guarantee. I nod so we can continue with our day.

"Sounds like a plan. I'll text Stacy and let her know we are ready for the first." Ryder shoots a text quickly on his phone then flips to a new page on his legal pad.

I'm not sure why he insists on paper while Alester and I switched to digital, but he refuses a tablet every time we offer him one. Stacy babies him and transfers all of his notes for him after each day and submits it to his main file hub. He better hope she never retires or he's screwed. We all are.

The day dragged on with our interviews, but we found the three main people we wanted to fill the secretary slots along with two extra that we may end up offering as well, after we check our plans and financials. The IT people were easy. A young woman and man fresh out of college and eager to set up a new company. They both have plans to stay in the city with plenty of hobbies, plus our pay and compensation make it an easy sell for them. We drafted a list of companies and individuals to go through next week for the other positions. Then we just need someone for marketing, to help promote our clients and make designs for us and them. That's the tricky part, artists are sometimes particular on things they want to make, and we want someone committed but free thinking.

Ryder follows me into my office and plops onto the couch with his notes. "Man, that was exhausting. Do you want to go out with me again? We can do dinner first. Maybe you can invite that hot chick from the other night." He raises his eyebrows at me suggestively.

"Sure, but I'm not inviting her because one, you're crazy and two, I don't have her number like I said. And we are going to that new brick oven pizza place, none of your weird restaurants." I power off my computer and grab my keys from inside the desk. I stand and put my jacket on. I should probably dig out my bigger coat for the weather coming tonight. An alert dings on my phone.

"Sold, I'll go get Alester." I follow behind him as he takes off towards Alester's office at the end of the hall.

The door is propped open when I get there. Alester faces five computer screens with various programs open on each as his eyes dart back and forth. "Hang on, I'm just finishing translating this search into multiple documents for you both to go through," Alester says.

Ryder is standing over his shoulder. "This is what your brain looks like before you organize it and send it to me? This shit is confusing. How do you even know what all of those letters and symbols mean?" Ryder scratches the back of his neck.

Alester continues to type as he answers Ryder. I lean against the doorway. "It's just a different language. The same as all of the finance programs are in a language that you understand, but I couldn't care less about any of that. We all have our strengths."

"Right, but money makes sense. This does not." Ryder starts tapping his foot. "Are you almost done? I'm starving and might start to chew on your arm if you don't hurry up."

Alester rolls his eyes but hits a collection of keys that shuts down every computer, one after another. "There. I'll just do it from home later."

"Yes! Let's go!" Ryder runs towards me, so I have to step out of the way.

"You're a child," I say.

"Eh, you like it." He laughs and runs to the elevator. "I'm going to whoop Alester's ass later in Call of Duty.

No working for him." He jumps in the elevator right as the doors open and tries to get the doors to close on us, but I jog over and shove my hand in the closing door.

"I don't think so. Not today." I hold the door for Alester.

"Asshole," Alester mumbles.

"I'll get you on Monday, just wait. It will be the stairs for the both of you."

Thomas is waiting with the SUV when we exit the elevator. I was about to send him a text, but he always just knows somehow. "Thomas, did you put a tracker on me?" I joke.

He smirks. "No, not you. Just the wild one." Thomas opens the back door, and I slide in. Alester climbs up front, he gets motion sickness and hates having to ride in the backseat. Ryder runs to the other side, not giving Thomas time to close one door before he's diving into the vehicle.

"You're extra hyper today," I comment.

"Just wait until I get my food." He wiggles his eyebrows at me.

*Fuck.*

We drape our jackets on the backs of our chairs before we sit down. The temperature is dropping quickly in preparation for this big storm they're promising. We aren't getting excited about it, though, because weathermen are notoriously wrong with every winter storm.

The waitress drops off our drink orders shortly after we sit down when Ryder starts hitting on her. Alester and I share a knowing look because this isn't out of the norm for him. We both tune him out, too used to the act he likes to put on.

Alester grunts and picks up his menu. I chuckle and pull out my phone, wishing I had a text from a certain someone who doesn't even have my number. *Stupid.*

"So," Ryder drags out when the waitress leaves to check on her other tables. "when are you going to ask out Alex, again?" Now he can remember her name.

I ignore Ryder and look at Alester. "Have any new dates coming up?"

He grunts again. "What is both of your obsession with dating all the time? You sound like a couple of teenage girls." He takes a long drink of his beer.

"Ryder started it," I grumble, looking for the waitress again so I can order my food.

"He's not exciting," Ryder huffs, turning to survey the room when his eyes light up. "But the fact that Alex and her friends just sat at that back booth is." He wiggles his eyebrows at me while I try to discreetly glance over my shoulder. Sure enough, she is in the booth with her two friends from the apartment. *Perfect.*

"Just leave them alone. They don't need your wild self in their space." The waitress notices me looking for her and makes her way over.

"What can I get you?" She pulls out her notepad and pen.

Ryder pounces. "Besides your number? We will take three large pepperoni and sausage pizzas. Oh! And an order of garlic bread." She laughs at Ryder, scribbles the order, then tears a portion of her page off and hands it to him before walking away. "Score." He slips it into his pocket. "So, I'm going to go say hi to Ashlyn, if you're not going to man up and head over there."

"Dude." Alester levels him with a glare.

*Jesus.* He starts to stand when I grab him. "Knock it off. I'll go. You keep your ass here."

"Ooooh, you're going! Yes! You can invite them to sit with us if you want. I don't mind."

I resist the urge to throttle him. "I don't think they need any of what you have to offer in their lives. Plus I have to get going soon."

"Ahh, yes. You can't just have time off like the rest of us. Always have to hustle." He takes a drink of his beer.

He tries to lean on Alester, but Alester shoves him away. "You could come back to the office and help me go through more applicants." Alester raises an eyebrow at him.

"Gross. It's half-day Friday. Not happening." Ryder scoffs and tries to act like his made-up schedule is a thing everywhere. He gets away with a lot, considering he finds most of the up-and-coming companies before they even think to find a marketing team. How he does it, we have no clue, but that's why he can do what he wants. Most of our profit starts with his boots on the ground, so to speak.

I slide off my seat and make my way to Alex's booth. I'm not sure why she makes me so nervous. It's not like I don't talk to women. I do. She just feels different, I guess. Like it could be more.

Their conversation screeches to a halt when I approach the table, three sets of eyes swinging towards me. "Sorry to interrupt, ladies." I turn and Alex's deep brown gaze locks me in place, like she can see through my soul. Her hair is piled in a bun on top of her head with tiny hairs escaping. "Alex, what are you ladies up to?" *Smooth, real smooth.* I'd kick myself if it wouldn't make things more awkward.

Her hand fiddles with her loose strands as she tries to tame them, to no avail. "Just taking a break from girls' day. What uh..."

"Oh! You should join us. I see the rest of your crew is here too!" Her friend Ashlynn is craning her neck to look at the guys behind me.

I try to tame my smirk, but it's no use. The universe is yanking us towards each other and I want nothing more than to launch into Alex's life, but I have a lot going on right now. It wouldn't be fair for her.

I watch as panic flashes through Alex's eyes, but the next moment it's gone and a shield is up as she forces a smile.

"I'm sorry," I say. "We would, but we are just getting a quick lunch before we have to go back to work. Next time."

I don't need to rush this, she obviously needs more time after everything with her ex, and I need to get my personal life in order. I can wait for her.

"Have a nice evening ladies. I'll see you soon, Alex." I wink at her.

*Fuck, why did I wink? That's such a douchy thing to do. Fuck.*

Thankfully the food is already at our table when I return, so I proceed to inhale my portion and throw a hundred on the table before bailing for work. I ignore Ryder's protests as Alester drags him out of the building and away from Alex and her friends.

Thank fuck for him, or Ryder would ruin every possible relationship I could have with his loud mouth and lack of filter.

# CHAPTER 10
## *Alexandra*

"I CAN'T BELIEVE James came to the pizza place too. Seems like you have a stalker." Ashlynn slides onto the new sofa and picks up her phone.

I try not to roll my eyes, but I'm pretty sure I fail. *What a laugh, me? Have a stalker? Yeah right. I can't even get a man to be faithful.*

"It's the best place for pizza. You know that, it's not that weird." I fiddle with my shirt, regretting my panic. I should have invited him to sit with us. I saw the hurt flash across his eyes before he hid it. Just like me, he doesn't show his pain. Two peas in a pod. I wonder what wounds he has hidden inside. Maybe he will tell me one day.

*No! No men for me until I figure out my job situation. Idiot.*

"Not to take you off subject, but if you really do plan

to leave us for the weekend or whatever, you should probably leave soon." Jaz shoves her phone in my face. She has the radar of Minnesota pulled up. I grab it from her hands and take in the large blue and purple blob making its way towards us a lot sooner than they initially said.

I scroll to the top and look at the hourly. *Shit.* It looks like it's going to get nasty, and quick. If I don't want to be stuck here in my apartment, I need to get out of here.

My phone dings from the table.

> Annabel: Have a great trip! I would be jealous if there was actual civilization there, but have fun none the less.
> Love you! Don't get murdered!
> Mwaaaaaa.

She's a dork. I grab my purse and open it, so I can start chucking my charger and snacks inside. "I better get everything loaded. I don't want to be stuck here and end up permanently jobless!"

I rush around grabbing my other bags. Jaz and Ashlyn help me carry everything to my car.

We hug goodbye before I get in the car to drive north.

Two hours into my four-hour drive, the snow is really starting to pick up. My little Toyota Camry is sliding everywhere. I've been meaning to upgrade to an all-wheel drive vehicle, but unfortunately my job doesn't pay enough for that upgrade. Well, I guess I should say didn't pay since now I'm jobless and *really* don't make any money. I've been trying to get promotions every year since being there, but it just never worked out.

I grip the wheel tighter and strain to see the lines as the snow covers more of the roadway. Every time I feel my tires sliding, I let off the gas and wait.

*I can't wait to get to the cabin, this is utterly exhausting.*

The radio is playing at a low volume as they interrupt for the weather announcement. "This highly anticipated storm is just starting. Travel is not advised at this time. We've got back-to-back storms hitting over the next few days and it will take time for plows to clean up the major interstates and even longer for residential roads..."

I about jump out of my skin when my phone's ringtone blares through the low voices of the weatherman on max volume. I quickly hit Answer on my steering wheel, not taking my eyes off the snowy road.

"Hello?"

"You aren't driving in this, are you? They say this will be the worst storm in a long time. Better just stay home." Mom's condescending tone echoes all around me. *God forbid I take a little time to figure out myself.*

I roll my eyes, but keep my voice neutral. "You must have talked to Annabel. I'm already over half-way, it will be fine. I'll keep going slow and get there eventually."

"Well…" She fumbles, flustered that I don't bend to her will, I imagine. "Well. Just be careful. If it gets too bad, you'll have to find somewhere to stay." Her tone gets higher in pitch as she tries to dictate more of my life. Each year she seems to be getting worse, ever since Dad left for his big European adventure. I feel bad that she's alone now. I just wish she would put all of her effort into her own life instead of trying to invade mine.

I huff out a breath, trying to keep my cool since I can barely see the lines on the road and I don't want to end up in the ditch. Especially while talking to my mom, that would be the real tragedy. "The plows are still out. Roads are fine, it's just coming down harder. It will be just fine. You worry too much. I've got to go though, you know, focus on driving. Love you, bye."

"Love you…."

I hit End Call before she can try to keep me on the phone.

Letting out a breath, I play some light tunes and focus on driving.

It takes an hour longer to get to the cabin than it should have, but when my GPS finally tells me to turn right on a tiny road surrounded by trees with snow covering the drive, I almost cry. *Great.*

I try not to slow down while correcting the car as it slides. I do *not* want to get stuck far away from the cabin and have to walk through all this shit. The single car-width-driveway starts to curve into a wider opening for parking but here the snow is piled even higher, causing my low-sitting car to slam to a stop.

I press the gas pedal harder. The car vibrates, snow flying in all directions, but I stay stationary. *Fuck.*

I shift into Reverse, hitting the gas. I try to rock the car to get more momentum to get through the snow, but I just dig myself in deeper.

I smack my hands against the steering wheel. "It's stuck. Great. I guess I'm walking from here." I groan looking at the knee-high snow I need to drag all my stuff through. I aggressively shove the car into Park. Definitely should have packed less or planned better. Let's be honest, neither of those options would have ever happened, but whatever.

I wiggle back into my coat, zipping it up to my chin and pull on my hat, gloves, and scarf. I can barely see with the sliver I've left myself between my hat and scarf, but my face will be warm.

I hike my purse over my shoulder and shove my door open as hard as I can, sliding out when I get a gap big enough to squeeze through. I trudge my way to the trunk, my socks and pants already soggy from the snow sticking to me. I want to throw myself a pity party for the large suitcase I decided to cram all my shit into or maybe just throw myself into a pile of snow and let it take me. My legs are already freezing.

Glancing at my route to the door, I can see where the owner had moved snow earlier. It's coming down so hard that the walkway is covered again, the level slightly less than where I'm currently stuck with my car blocking the entire driveway.

I heft my bag into the snow and start pulling it through to the walkway. I'm no longer cold by the time I get to the wrap-around porch. Breathing heavily, I hunch over my bag handle to give myself a moment to breath in the humid air coating my face from my scarf.

*I made it!* I'm wet everywhere, either from sweat or snow, lucky me. I need a shower after this, or a bath with wine.

The smell of a fire burning mixes with the frigid air whipping around me outside. Glancing up through the falling snowflakes, I see the lights on through the cabin windows and smoke billowing through the chimney. I soak up every piece of the sight, from the way the light streams through the windows, to the trees surrounding it, covered in an even layer of snow. If I could reach my phone, I'd take a photo, but I'll just have to burn it into my brain for now.

A sigh escapes me. I can't wait to get inside and curl under every soft blanket stocked in the cabin after I'm clean. "I. Hate. Winter."

I stand at the bottom of the steps, trying to figure out how I'm going to climb them with my giant bag without falling. I decide to leave my bag at the bottom of the steps and at least get the door open. I climb the stairs, knocking the snow off my shoes the best I can along the way. I jiggle the doorknob, but it's locked. A keypad sits above the handle, mocking me.

"Shit. What was that stupid code I was emailed?" I slap my hands on my pockets looking for my phone. Of course I wouldn't put it somewhere easy. I rip my purse off my shoulder and open it.

"I thought I heard someone out here," a man's voice says.

I scream and throw my purse at him on instinct.

"Shit. Sorry. I didn't mean to scare you."

I blink, my eyes heavy with snowflakes. Everything is blurry from the steam of my breath coming up from my scarf. The voice sounds familiar, but I can't pinpoint where in my soggy state. I look down as I try to hide my face from the wind.

"Let me get that bag for you, so you can warm up inside."

I hesitate. "Why are you here? Am I at the wrong cabin?" *Please don't be that because my car is not going to move.* I rub my eyes and try to figure out what is happening. I look up at his face and stutter. "What the fuck? James! What are you doing at my cabin?"

He squints at me like I'm crazy, but then I realize he can't see what I look like given my entire face and body are covered in winter gear. I throw my hat and scarf off.

"Alex? Uh. That's not what my reservation said..."

"*Your* reservation?" I ask as I stomp into the cabin. I'm over the snow. He follows me, softly closing the door behind him.

I throw my soggy coat on a hook by the door and kick my shoes off. There's not much I can do about the pants at this moment.

James's eyebrows pinch in confusion. "Yes," he drags out. "I own this cabin. I got behind with my other obligations and lost track of time. By the time I got out here to set everything up the plows had been removed and they were announcing everyone needed to stay indoors. I knew you already left from your messages, so I figured I would stay to ensure you made it safely."

"What if I didn't make it here?"

James shrugs. "I would have called in the name you

registered with, but I guess that wouldn't have helped since it didn't say Alexandra." He gives me a pointed stare. "Where the hell does Janise come from?"

I groan, feeling like an idiot, and also what in the actual fuck is happening? I hide my face in my hands. "I use my middle name when booking things because I watch too many documentaries about serial killers, okay? Sue me! How is this your rental? How many fucking jobs do you have!" I literally just quit mine and have no clue what I'm going to do and this guy has like twenty jobs going at the same time.

I watch his face as he processes my reaction. He blinks a few times then shrugs. "I like to stay busy. I'm going to grab your bag and bring it in." He slides out the front door and is back within a minute with my snow covered suitcase by his side. *Shit.*

James reaches into the entryway closet, grabs a towel, and lays it on the floor before placing my wet bag on top. I watch him glimpse at me huddled by the fire before he makes his way to the kitchen in the corner. "I made some coffee and hot chocolate. I wasn't sure which you would prefer after your drive."

I almost melt, thinking about the warm drinks, my irritation *mostly* forgotten. "Half of each, together, actually sounds amazing. Thank you."

"Odd, but I'll allow it."

He gets to work filling a mug while I stare into the flames and slowly defrost.

When he hands me the mug, I smile. The giant pile

of whipped cream on top makes me giddy and the chocolatey aroma lights me up from the inside.

James sits on the two-seater sofa across from me before continuing, "This cabin has been in the family for generations. I don't like the idea of letting it sit empty over the winter, so I rent it out occasionally. Although not a lot of people like to book a cabin in the woods with no Wi-Fi, so it's not very busy." He crosses his arms and leans back. "Why *did* you book a cabin in the woods with no Wi-Fi?"

I tentatively take a sip of my warm concoction and let out a light moan. "Sooo good." I lick the layer of cream off my top lip and I peer through my lashes at him. His eyebrows are raised as he zones in on my mouth. "Oops." I look back at the fire as I feel my cheeks flush from my inappropriate mouth. "Anywho. I needed some space to think, to paint, to just breathe without anything interrupting me. I need to figure out what I'm doing next, since I quit my job last wee—."

*Fuck.* I wasn't going to tell him that. Why did I tell him that? Fucking fireplace and amazing coffee-cocoa. I blame you.

He nods as if I'm not a total nut-case. "Well, the place is yours. I'm going to try to get out of here before I'm stuck for good. There's a master bedroom down the hall with a large claw foot tub that I'm sure you will enjoy after the cold." He stands and goes to the door, putting on his coat and boots, since he was apparently smart enough to dress for the weather, unlike me.

I fumble to stand, my legs groaning in my wet pants. I collect myself before he can notice my wince and make my way over. "Thank you for everything, really. I can't believe you own this place, but I'm glad it's you and not some creep." He smirks, making me blush again as I mumble. "Be safe out there, it wasn't great on my way in."

"I'll be fine. I grew up here, so I'm used to it." He flashes a full smile at me before heading out the door.

I deflate my body. Everything is aching as I make my way to the end of the hall with my suitcase. I open the door and let out a quiet squeal. The king-size bed in the center of the room with a cream-colored comforter and enough pillows to swim in looks like heaven. There's a long bench seat against windows that climb the entire length of the wall to the ceiling, showcasing the woods out back with its fresh snowfall. It's beautiful. I wheel my bag by the closet and make my way to the master bathroom. Opening the door, a gasp leaves my lips. *He wasn't kidding.* The bathtub is huge. It could easily fit two or even three people inside.

The smell of freshly washed towels slaps me in the face, but I love the lavender smell mixed with pine in the air. I take in the fluffy robes and folded towels draped next to the large claw foot tub with a tray off to the side to hold whatever I would want with me.

My fingers brush over the buttery soft material as my eyes catch on a plate of products. "What's this?" I reach over and pick up a few. Winter scent bubble bath, Vanilla scent bubble bath, soaps, shampoos, conditioner, oils... the list goes on with more next to the sink that I will have to investigate later.

I open the winter scent and bring it to my nose, the light aroma of pine trees in the chilly fall air when snow is just about to fall surrounds me. My favorite. I reach over and turn the hot water knob on the tub and put a few scoops of bubble bath in. While I wait for that to fill, I go into the bedroom to unpack my limited clothing.

I hang my inappropriate clothing that's not suited for the current weather raging outside and stuff my bag in the bottom of the closet. I grab my phone off the bed and start my soothing playlist. A notification from Mom lights up my screen. I peek in at the tub and rush to turn it off before reading my latest message.

> Mom: Be safe. Try to meet someone! I'm not getting any younger and neither are you. Love you.

"Great." I swipe the messages closed and notice the corner of my phone flashing. "Oh, look, one bar, *barely.*"

I set my phone to airplane mode. I don't need it to die mid bath while it searches for more bars, plus I need a full break. No more messages from mom. I need my music to float around me while I blissfully ignore all my life choices.

Twisting my hair on top of my head, I strip and slide under the scalding water. "This is already the best trip I've been on. A whole week of this is just what I need."

I don't turn off the nozzle until the water is above my shoulders. My body is completely covered in warmth, the scent of trees wrapping around me. I hear a dull thud from far away, but I'm sure it's just the logs from the fireplace settling. I brush it off as I relax into the heat and close my eyes.

After being in the tub for an hour and refilling it twice, I slip from the water and slide the fluffy robe over my body. Next step, find my cozy socks, get a bottle of wine, and relax by the fire. I was able to stuff every pair of fluffy socks I own in my bag without Ashlyn noticing. I hate having cold feet. Sweat drips down my back and chest from staying in water so hot it turned my skin pink. I slide the sides of my robe open to let in a little breeze, the tie barely holding it all together. *That's better.*

The listing said the cabin came stocked with limited wine and beer, so I leave the few bottles I packed on the dresser and open the bedroom door. The warm scent of blueberry muffins and coffee wafts through the air. "Mmmm, I could definitely get used to this." Closing my eyes, I take a deep breath, letting the aroma lift me up. A memory rushes to the surface.

*Ten-year-old me stands in the kitchen at my grandma's house. Fresh coffee drips into the pot as Grandma reaches for a mug. "Alexandra, would you like a cup?"*

*I lift my face away from the strawberries and powdered sugar I'm eating, my brown eyes wide. "Um, yes!" I squeal, bouncing in my seat. Mom would never allow me coffee.*

*My grandma laughs and pours me half a cup, then pulls out the milk and sugar and sets it next to my mug. I rush over to look inside. "It will be hot. Add some milk." My grandma smiles as she takes her own cup, full and black, sipping and watching me.*

*I dump milk in, filling the cup almost to the top, and take a big sip. "Ew. I don't like it." I scrunch my nose in disgust and set it down.*

*She laughs again and slides the sugar to me with a spoon, nodding to my cup.*

*I add three large spoonfuls, stir, and sip again. My nose scrunches again, but now I'm determined. It's getting better but still not great. I add four more scoops, stir, and sip. A slow smile spreads across my little face. Grandma smiles back and waves me over. "Okay. Let's make blueberry muffins."*

*I slowly walk over to the bowl, watching my coffee cup closely so it doesn't slosh all over the floor, and set it next to the mixing bowl.*

A man's throat clearing snaps me out of my memory. "I definitely could, too." I jump as James's eyes bore into mine, searing my soul before he looks back at the oven and turns the timer off before it can beep. He pulls out the tray of muffins as I stare, trying to get my mind to catch up.

"Umm...what are you still doing here?" My breathing is erratic as I watch the muscles on his forearms flex where his sleeves are rolled up. He slides his hands slowly into the front pockets of his jeans, which are hugging everything perfectly, and I mean *everything* as he leans against the counter. *Did it get hotter in here?*

I run my hand over my neck as my eyes travel back up to his face. Those eyes simmer with a hunger I haven't seen...in, well...a long time. I glance down to see what he's looking at and see the curve of my breasts breaking out from where the robe hangs open. *Oops.* I slowly slide the sides together and pull the tie tight, suddenly suffocating again.

James keeps his eyes glued to mine. "It's worse than I initially thought out there. Your car is also stuck in the middle of the driveway, so I will have to clear it out in the morning when I can see better." He places a muffin and a full cup of coffee-cocoa in front of me. "I'll sleep on the couch, so I won't bother you. But unfortunately, you're stuck with me tonight."

My cheeks flush even further knowing I'm part of the reason he's stuck with me. "I'm sorry. I didn't think anyone would be here, and I couldn't see where to park... Not that my car was going much further, stupid thing gets stuck in the smallest amount of snow..."

I'm rambling. I didn't expect him to be here when I arrived, let alone hours later, and *now*, he's staying the night.

*This is a complete disaster.* Hopefully my trip of reflection won't be completely ruined and James can get back to his life soon.

"Alex?" My head snaps up. James's eyes are still trying to sear through to my soul.

*Shit.* I'm in my head again. "Uh, yeah. That's fine. I mean, what else are you going to do with this weird storm?" I shrug and shove part of the hot muffin in my mouth. There's nothing better than a muffin straight out of the oven.

This is totally the most normal thing that could happen to two people that are basically strangers-slash-fake dating to *certain* people. I'm not nervous at all to have a very sexy man that happens to be an amazing kisser snowed in with me.

He nods and glances behind me. "Would you like to sit by the fire with your snack?"

I agree on reflex as he collects the plate of muffins and his coffee before heading to the table in the living room.

I inhale a shaky breath, gathering myself before turning to follow him. *I should have put clothes on. Fucking idiot.* Too late now, I guess.

I scurry to the chair across from him. I set my mug

down and grab a fuzzy blanket from the basket in the corner and wrap it around my body. It's already warm by the fire and under this robe, but I really don't need to flash James...again. Honestly, the amount of dumb shit he's witnessed from me at this point is astonishing and should show him enough red flags to run for the hills.

# CHAPTER 11
## James

SITTING in front of the fireplace with Alex wrapped in the robe I picked out is pure torture, even with her trying to cover her body in that fluffy blanket. I can see her at war with herself. Her eyes keep darting to me and back down to her drink. That's okay. I'm a patient man. I have the time, but that doesn't mean that I can't help her figure out what she wants. *Me.* I mean what else are we going to do while we're stuck in this cozy cabin together? The snow is raging outside in a storm escalating to an effect they haven't seen in decades. At least that's what the news broadcast said when I tried to leave in my truck. The tree coverage around this place blocks a lot of wind and snow, and we are still getting dumped on. I can't imagine what it's like on the open road.

Alex leans closer to pick up another muffin. I latch onto her eyes like it's the last time we will ever see each other. "So, why the cabin in the woods? I don't see you as the outdoorsy type. There had to be other no-wifi places, or you could just turn off your phone." I say, knowing damn well I don't do any of the shit I'm preaching. The only way to keep me from working is by making it impossible for me to actually do the work. The red creeping up her neck and coloring her cheeks does something to me. I want to see it every day.

"Well, I'm not." She looks down, picking at the wrapper around the muffin before continuing. "I liked the isolated aspect. No one to reach out to me, spotty cell service..." Her shoulders drop and she lets out a breath. "I quit everything in my life, and I need to see if I can dig myself out of it. But I can't do that with all the noise of the world. So, your posting was just what I needed."

I nod, taking her in. The pain reflecting in her eyes vanishes as she puts a wall back up. It makes sense. Whatever she's searching for, and I want her to find it. Maybe I could help in some way. My wheels start turning, picturing all the people I know and the opportunities I could present to her. But I would need to find a way to do it anonymously. I don't like people knowing what I have and what I do. I've been burned too many times.

"Why do you rent this place? Just so it doesn't stay empty seems like a cop-out. You obviously have money, from whatever you do for the Edward Corporation. Couldn't you and your cousins just use it?"

*Smart.* She's smart. This is trouble. It's making me like her even more, if that's possible.

I take a long drink before answering her. I didn't

think we'd get here yet, but I'm also not going to lie to her. "You're right." I run a hand through my hair. "Look, not many people know about this, so I'd love it if you kept it to yourself."

Alex leans forward but keeps her lips tightly sealed.

"This is…" I pause, trying to gather how to say this to someone who didn't know him. "*Was* my dad's favorite place. His parents passed it to him, and he would bring me here as a child as much as he could. He couldn't come as much as he wanted towards the end." I blink away the memories trying to take over. "I like to allow others to experience it, since he can't."

I stop. I can't keep talking about him to someone who didn't know him. Or that I don't know as well. I like Alex. I can see a future with her if she's open to it eventually. Maybe then I'll tell her all about my dad.

I jump when I feel her gentle touch on my arm. I didn't even notice her crossing over to the couch I'm sitting on. I look up into her deep brown eyes, and I'm home.

"I'm so sorry. This place really is beautiful. Thank you for sharing it with me."

I brush a piece of hair behind her ear. I can't stop myself. It's like an out-of-body experience, but she doesn't pull away. She stays. A soft sigh leaves her lips, those lips I haven't been able to stop thinking about since that night at the club. It feels like ages ago, but here she is rooting herself into my life without even trying. It feels as if she's always been mine. Time has finally caught up and showed her to me, and now ... Now I can't let her go.

My hand slides around to the back of her neck. Before I can stop myself I'm pulling her towards me. Her sweet inhale and fluttering eyelids are all I need before my lips crash to hers. I almost groan at the taste of her, chocolate with the hint of blueberry, but then her own unique vanilla overloading my senses as I sweep my tongue past her lips. Her hands grip my sweater, pulling me closer still. I gently lean her against the couch as I explore her beautiful mouth. My hands stay on her neck and hip, not pushing this further, even with every strain against my zipper.

I pull back, taking in her sparkling brown eyes, red cheeks, and plump lips. Her whine of protest has me chuckling.

"What's so funny?" Her lust filled voice does things to me. I want nothing more than to slowly peel that fluffy robe from her body, but I don't want her to feel forced into this situation since I shouldn't be here to begin with.

I run my thumb over her bottom lip, and her mouth opens for me. *Damn.* That mouth alone could bring me to my knees. "Nothing. Nothing at all. You're perfect." I lay my head back and watch her.

She huffs and sits up, curling her legs beneath her. She hums. "Well, if I'm so perfect, then why did you stop?"

I take her hand in mine, kissing her palm. "Baby, I

don't ever want to stop, but that isn't what your vacation is about. I'm not going to hijack that from you. I just couldn't resist tasting you again with you so close to me."

Alex's cheeks flush at my comment, her eyes darting from her hand and back to me. "But..." She blinks. "*Baby?* What is happening?"

I laugh again. I can't help it. She's literally a dream and she can't even see it. "Yes, because however much time it takes, I don't care how long. You *will* be mine. It's inevitable. *We* are inevitable. I've known since that night in the club." She stares at me, and I throw another smirk her way, knowing she loves to hate it. "I'm a patient man. I know what I want when I see it, and *you* are everything I've ever wanted. I just didn't know you yet. Now that I do, there's no going back for me."

"This is crazy." She shakes her head, but she doesn't pull away. Alex snuggles closer into the couch, her body still inches from mine. She picks at her nails. "If you already know I'm *yours* then why wait?"

It's my turn to let out an exhale because sometimes being a good guy is torture, but at least I'm just torturing myself. "As much as I want you. *Trust me*. You could have me whenever you want. I want to make sure you're in the right headspace. You've been through a lot in a short time. I don't want to rush this for you. I'd rather move at your pace, learn more about each other."

"Okay. Fine. I agree to your terms." She reaches over my lap to the table, grazing me with her breasts. She grabs her mug and settles back, batting her eyes at me like she doesn't know what she just did.

*Alright, this is going to be fun. My little minx.* "You first."

Alex crosses one leg over the other, causing her robe to fall open. I take the opportunity to slide my hand onto her thigh, right above her knee. I draw slow circles on her soft skin. "Where are you from?" I ask her. I know most of the public knowledge about her. After Alester met Alex he couldn't help but do a deep dive without me having to ask. He sent it to me right after he collected it, but what he can't find is the *why* she did the things she did, the personal reasoning behind things. Why does a person move or stay in a location? Did they have a good upbringing? They can track everything on social media, but for those people like Alex who don't post personal information, I can't learn as much.

Her eyes are glued to my hand, so I slide it a little further. Still a respectable distance, but it does the trick and causes her to squirm in her seat. I squeeze her thigh a little to get her attention back to me. "Right," she says as she clenches her legs together. "I'm, uh, from here. Well, not this far north, but near Shadowbrook, just a smaller town."

I grunt. "This isn't going to be helpful, if you don't open up to me." She looks down again, so I squeeze her leg. "I want to know everything, Alex. The good and the bad. Why'd you leave your home town? What do you want in life?"

Sucking her bottom lip into her mouth she stares at her lap. "I left because I wasn't going to be able to live in that environment any longer. I knew the best option for my health and longevity would be to get out. Experience something new, meet new people. Work on my art. I went to school for art and marketing while working a job I didn't love because my parents didn't agree with my life choices. I haven't had extra money to do anything other than pay for my schooling and additional classes to try to make it in life." Alex finally lifts her eyes to me. She looks as if a weight has been lifted. "Being in the city is like a fresh start. It's not too far from my sister who is going to school at the university an hour from me, but it's not embedded in my old memories. My mom goes to all of her events here, and my dad is, well, off reinventing himself, so who knows where exactly. Shadowbrook has more opportunities, and my friends are here. They're my family." She twirls a strand of hair while I take in everything she's telling me.

"When did you meet Ashlyn and Jaz?"

Now she smiles. "Well, Ashlyn used to live in my building. Before she bought a fixer upper that Jaz has adopted herself onto for free rent while she's in school." She laughs. "She saw my sister and I dragging my few boxes up the stairs to the third floor and offered to help in her ridiculous shoes. She almost fell down the stairs at one point, but I was behind her and pushed against her with a box in my arms. Ash is the kind of person you just gravitate towards. She's a hyper ball of energy, but she's been through the ringer. The things she's been through make her extreme with who she allows in her space. Jaz, we found her in our favorite coffee shop. She was carrying a huge stack of textbooks looking for a table. Of course it was packed, so Ash being Ash stole a chair from a table full of frat-bros and called her over. We've been stuck with each other ever since."

I love listening to her talk. I could just lay here all night, while she tells me every tale of her life. "I love that, I'm glad you found the family that you needed. I'm sorry you had to find it the hard way, but sometimes those relationships last longer than the ones we are born into."

"Okay. My turn. Have you always lived here? I've never seen you at Club X before that night." Alex crosses her arms and stares me down. It's probably the cutest thing I've ever seen.

"Tough question. I grew up in Faith, Minnesota, but I went to college in New York." I run my hand through my hair. "I came to Shadowbrook for business...and to see if I want to stay." That line hangs in the air. An opening to see if this is something she may want to give a chance to or not.

"From New York to this little city." Alex chuckles. "You seem to have all of the resources to travel the world and live anywhere, yet you're thinking of choosing this place?"

"I need to make more time for what's left of my family, or at least try. But a certain someone is making the decision to stay easier every day."

# CHAPTER 12
## *Alexandra*

MY HEART SKIPS. James makes me want to throw my hesitations out the window. He's been through so much in his life already, yet he wants to add my mess to the mix. "My turn. Tell me about your all-time favorite relationship you've had."

"Easy." He smirks. "It hasn't happened yet." James watches me with an intensity that has me squirming in my robe.

Heat travels up my neck and blazes over my cheeks. "Right. Okay. Your turn."

He taps his chin. "What's your biggest turn on in a man?"

My face feels like it's on fire. I'm one more comment away from launching myself into a pile of snow outside. "I don't think I should answer that." I pick at my fingers in my lap, avoiding his gaze.

James chuckles and takes a drink from his mug, the

aroma from the still-steaming cocoa invading my senses. "Alright, alright. What else do you want to know?"

I chance a peek from my lashes and immediately regret it. How am I supposed to resist that? His cream sweater without a wrinkle in sight is making his green eyes pop in the firelight. The woodsy smell clings to him like he was made for it. I'm fighting my body's urge to lean into him. Into the moment.

*Wait. Am I already falling into the trap that he says we are inevitable? Maybe.*

I need to stop being such a relationship hopper. Maybe he'd be fine with just having a good time for now. Or maybe it's time I take a page out of Ash's book and avoid relationships. It's not like they've been working for me lately.

I grind my lip through my teeth, trying to go over my life options, and my eyes dart back to James. His eyes are locked on my mouth. I release my lip with a pop. "What?"

His gaze jumps to mine. "If you keep biting your lip like that, we might have to speed up the timeline."

My cheeks flush further. "How can you confidently just let that shit slip out of your mouth?"

James leans close, his lips grazing my neck. I resist the urge to gravitate closer yet. My arousal is radiating off me. I suppressing a whimper and rub my legs together to try to ease some of the ache.

"I'm barely controlling myself around you," he whispers, "so worrying about what my mouth says is the least of my worries. I can't stop thinking about that mouth, ever since our first kiss."

My head turns involuntarily towards him. We're inches apart, but he's not moving. He's waiting to see what I will do next, but I have no fucking clue how we even got to this point. My heart is pounding in my head. He has to be able to hear it, if not feel it vibrating the air around us. My mind is waging war on my body at hyper speed. *Is it too soon? Does time matter when you're cheated on? What if this all ends tomorrow? What if it's only temporary?*

But then the loudest voice comes through the chaos. '*Life is short, babygirl. It can all be gone in an instant. Be bold. Make the choices that scare you the most.*' My grandma. She was wild and free. She never regretted changing careers or who she chose in life, even if she was broke at times. She always said living was worth it because she watched enough people die before they did anything worthwhile.

James's mouth curls up on one side like he has me all figured out, his pine scent wrapping around me like a warm hug. My mind goes silent as I slowly lean closer, gently brushing my lips against his. Just a whisper of a kiss that sets my life on fire before I pull back. My eyes flutter open as I take in the sliver of green still showing in his. *Oops. I think I pushed him too far.*

His lips crash into mine, his hands tangling into my hair at the nape of my neck. A moan slips from my lips as I brace my hands on his chest. We take our time exploring each other, but yet it ends too quickly. We pull apart. I'm not sure who did it first, but slowly I blink up at him like he didn't just upend my entire existence with a kiss.

He's still looking at me with those eyes. The ones that want to eat me alive. "You should go before things escalate."

I wipe my sweaty palms on my robe. "Yeah. I...I should go to my room."

I push off the couch, taking my mug with me. I turn to tell him goodnight when I notice his gaze hasn't left me, and neither has the intense look in them while he's looking down at the robe I'm in. I look down. *Fucking thing*. It's parted again. James isn't getting a full show, but it definitely isn't PG. I huff and take off down the hall. I need to get clothes on before this goes right where he said he wasn't ready for it to.

I make it to my door and shut it quickly behind me like I'm being chased. Obviously, James isn't following, but why do I wish he had?

*No, stop it.* We can make it through one night without me trying to rip his clothing off like a teenager. I just need to redirect my energy into my art. Yeah, that's it.

I rush to the closet and pull on shorts and a tank top. Why did I let Ashlyn pack my bag? *Ugh.* It seemed like such an empowering moment, explore my sexuality, free myself. *Yeah, great.* These shorts barely cover my ass, so I guess I'm stuck in my room for the rest of the night.

I start digging out my paints and a fresh canvas. Unfolding my compact easel, I place it near the large window and drag the nightstand over, so I can use it as a table for my supplies. After I have everything organized the way I like, I squeeze out some white, black, and blue paint to start my background. The second my brush glides across the page I'm lost. The noise fades away, the thoughts blissfully drift into their boxes. I let out a breath and really let myself go to the process.

I am halfway through the background when the lights flicker, then go out completely. *Shit.*

# CHAPTER 13

## James

"WHO DOESN'T HAVE a generator for a house in the woods?" Alex crosses her arms in front of her chest, which only causes the tiny strappy thing she's wearing to allow more of her breasts to spill from the silk material.

"I mean, I have an old small one, but it's only big enough to power the fridge. I've been meaning to get a bigger one, but I've been a little busy lately..."

I try to focus on adding more logs to the fire to avoid staring at her, but she's so distracting. Especially after tasting her, I won't be getting her out of my head anytime soon. I told myself I would wait, but I'm apparently a weak man when it comes to Alexandra. She flooded my system all at once, and none of my nerve endings wanted to be without her. They still don't, but I want to make sure this is something she really wants. With everything else she's been through, I can't be selfish, yet. Dad always told me to get out and live. I couldn't just take care of him or work the rest of my days, but I haven't let myself trust anyone enough to follow his orders. Nothing feels difficult with Alex, but maybe that's my dick talking. *Can't trust that guy.* "It will be fine, I'm sure the city will have it back up in no time."

She scrunches her nose like she doesn't believe a word I say. "What are we supposed to do until then?"

"Well..." I wave my hand at the fire I've been tending. "We will have to move your bed into the living room for the night, since the walls aren't that insulated to keep you warm through tomorrow. I'll stay up and make sure the fire keeps going, and in the morning, I will have to bring more wood in for the rest of your stay." Alex fidgets with her shirt, unsure. "Does that sound okay?"

I don't want to spook her, but there aren't any other options. We are essentially cut off until they can move the snow and fix the power.

She sighs. "I guess I'll get the blankets." She trudges down the hall into the room. I try really hard not to watch her walk away, but my eyes can't stop their pull towards everything about her. It's like they're dying of thirst and Alex is the finest wine around. They won't stop drinking her in every chance they can get.

I clear the furniture from the center of the room, pressing the couch and chairs to the walls, then grab the mattress and lay it on the rug near the fireplace, but not too close in case a stray log decides to jump out. Alex goes back to the room when I start arranging the blankets and pillows on the bed. She returns a moment later carrying an easel, wet canvas, and paints. She starts setting it up just so on the side of the fireplace, making multiple trips back to the bedroom to bring out more supplies. By the time she's done, it looks like a mini art studio has been set up.

"So, this is what you planned to do while you were here?"

She sits on her stool, picking up her brush before she looks at me. "You sound surprised." She flourishes her arms at her tiny tank and shorts not suitable for painting. "Do I not look like a painter?"

She holds my stare without laughing or smiling, and I'm not sure if she's offended or if she really believes that outfit makes her look like a painter. I run my hand over the stubble starting to grow. "Well … that's not something I would choose to paint in per se."

Alex blinks at me a few times. I'm starting to sweat under the stare, but then she breaks and doubles over laughing. "Oh my gosh. Your face." She sucks in air. "You look like you're going to pass out. I was kidding." She wipes at a stray tear. "Ashlyn." she points at herself. "She insisted on packing my bags and said it would be a healthy experience to free my sexuality."

My shoulders relax. *Thank God.* "She wants you to experience painting in the nude then?" My imagination is in overdrive and it's causing blood to travel to places it shouldn't.

Red creeps up her neck and across her cheeks, and it's beautiful. She's beautiful. "Um, I mean, yeah. I think so, but I can't do that with you here, now can I?" She spreads out the paints before she dips the brush in and starts sliding it across the canvas.

"I wouldn't mind, but I'm not going to be pushy." I make my way around to see the canvas. So far, it's a mixture of blues and grays. "What is it?"

She looks over her shoulder at me. "It's a background. You'll have to wait and see what the final product is." She turns, dipping her brush in more paint before adding more depth to various areas. "If I let you see it."

I laugh at that. I don't think anyone has told me I can't do something since the company took off. They all just want to throw ideas and work at me to see if I can make them rich overnight. Not that that's exactly what happened with our company, but that's all outsiders seem to see. Or women who want me for my money. Like my ex, Rebecca. "I have a feeling you'll let me by the end."

"Cocky. Good thing you won't be here to find out, since you're leaving in the morning." She sends me a pointed look.

Shaking my head, I make my way out the door to grab the generator, gas can, and an extension cord for the fridge, while she gets lost in her work. I'll be seeing all of her paintings eventually because she will be mine. I can see her sharp edges softening. She wants to open up. She just doesn't trust herself yet.

I feel a dip in the mattress and rub my eyes. I must have dozed off while Alex was painting. "Sorry. What time is it?"

Alex slides under the blankets and pulls them up to her chin. She's shivering. "Uh, late. I'm not sure." I can hear her teeth chatter together, her body shaking the mattress.

I look over at the mini vintage grandfather clock near the fireplace and see it's two in the morning. I glance at the fire. Shit. It's down to embers. I get up and stack more logs within the cage, watching as the dry wood catches fire from the coals. *That should last us until the morning.* I settle back in the bed when I'm done and hold the blankets open. "Come over here."

Alex looks adorable, tucked in her little burrito, but her lack of clothing isn't helping her at the moment. "I don't think we should cross that line," she mumbles through the blanket, still shaking.

I growl at her and tug her towards me. She yelps but doesn't fight it. "You're freezing. I'm not going to let you sit over there and shiver. Now that I know about what you've packed for clothing, I'm not going to be able to leave until the power is back *and* the roads are plowed."

She hums in response. I'm going to take that as an agreement. Her shaking is slowing as my body heat bleeds into her. I wrap my arms around her waist and thread my legs through hers, so we are touching everywhere. I refuse to leave her here in the middle of nowhere without everything she possibly needs.

Her shivering fully stops as she nuzzles in closer to my body. Her scent of vanilla floods my senses. I want to take a deep inhale of her hair, but that would be weird. Instead, I rest my chin on top of her head and squeeze her tighter, ensuring she's stuck for the night, and listen to her breathing even out as she falls asleep.

I wake up to the sun streaming through the large windows. Alex is still tucked in my arms, sound asleep. My arm is numb, but I slowly slide it out from under her as stealthily as possible. She rolls onto her stomach but stays in a deep sleep. I watch her for a moment. Her hair is spread all over the pillow. I watch her mouth as she mumbles something in her sleep that I can't catch. My mouth turns up in the corner. I could stand here and watch her sleep all day, but I need to check the weather and clear the snow. I turn, making my way to the front door and slide my boots and coat on.

I open the front door and stop. The snow is piled up in the doorway to almost half the height. And it's *still* snowing. *What in the hell?*

I quietly click the door shut, checking that I didn't wake Alex before going to the back door. It opens without an issue, the tree coverage providing additional wind protection from the storm. I check the small generator powering the fridge and topping it off with gas before I pull my gloves on and trudge my way through the snow to the shed.

I swing the door in and hop over the mound of snow to try and keep as much of it out of the building as possible. I prop the doors open for outside light, and I make my way to the workbench searching for the old radio I keep in case the power goes out. It has a solar power plate, so it's perfect for this little getaway that is prone to power outages in bad weather. Hopefully it still has a little charge left.

I find it buried under old newspapers left from when my dad would come out here to tinker on machines and walk the property. I must have stacked the papers on the radio the last time I was in the shed. I keep trying to come out and get rid of his things, slowly. But even with all of this time passing, it's still really hard to accept that I'll never see him walk through that door. He won't ever get to experience a night at this cabin again. He's gone. *I miss him.*

I shake off the thoughts and turn on the radio, scanning for the local station and wait for the signal to stabilize.

"—we expect this storm to continue to dump snow all through the weekend. The plows have been pulled and won't be out until Monday morning. For the safety of everyone, please stay home. Rescue teams are having trouble getting to cars that are sliding into ditches and getting stuck in snow-drifts. Many areas are without power. Companies are working to get lines fixed if they are able. If you are in a dire situation, call the emergency line. They are waiting to help families in need. We will continue to monitor the storm's impact and make adjustments when possible."

I turn the dial off to save power and prop the solar side up facing the window to try to charge. I guess I'm snowed in a bit longer. Hopefully Alex is okay with me staying since we don't have a choice. I'll have to refund her account when my phone is powered back up. We have plenty of wood to last all weekend, so that shouldn't be a problem. If necessary, I can go chop up a few of the downed trees in my woods for more. Luckily, the cabin is small. The fireplace should keep the internal pipes warm enough so they don't freeze.

I check that my gas cans are full, top off my snow-blower, and slide the shed's garage door open. Time to get to work moving some of this snow from the cement slab and front steps. Otherwise I won't be able to move it later.

It took a few hours, but I cleared off the entire deck and cement slab between the cabin and shed. Unfortunately, the snow is still coming down really hard, and my work is quickly getting covered again. *At least I can use the front door again to bring more firewood inside.*

I start moving wood from the pile by the shed to the deck to make it easier to feed the fire. By the time I'm finished, I'm drenched in so much sweat that the cold isn't even affecting me anymore. After stacking enough wood to get us through the night again, I knock my boots off on the steps and head back inside the cabin.

I glance to the fire first, noting that Alex has been feeding it extra logs since she got up. The blankets are made neatly on the bed. I scan to the kitchen, finally smelling the eggs and bacon cooking on the gas stove. My stomach grumbles loudly, causing Alex to peek over her shoulder. Her dark brown hair flows down her back. I'm absolutely captivated by this woman. I don't know what's wrong with me. I take in every inch of her from her dark eyes to her hair covering her tiny tank top that barely covers much of her skin to the silk shorts. The hem of the shorts is dangerously close to sliding up her cheeks.

*Damn. She's going to wreck me.*

I clear my throat and instead of confessing all the crazy thoughts flying through my head, I say, "It smells delicious. I'm going to rinse off quick."

Alex nods and goes back to cooking. Even though I don't have a generator big enough to power the entire cabin, I was at least smart enough to have gas appliances and a manual pump put in for the well. I need to make a note to pick up a larger generator to power the entire cabin or at least invest in some lanterns.

I am enjoying not being connected to my phone, though. Thank God I don't have to see Ryder's incessant messages throughout the day. He's probably having a panic attack that the texts aren't being opened. Poor Alester. He will have his hands full.

I turn the water to scalding and switch it to the shower-head. The claw foot tub is nice, but sometimes I just want a quick shower. I grab a fresh towel from under the sink and notice Alex's products strewn all over the counter like she lives here. I slide her tube of makeup further onto the counter, so it doesn't roll off, and smile. This is her, the messy artist side. She's too busy thinking about the piece she keeps rushing to in the living room to worry about what she leaves behind. I love seeing these mundane parts of her, the parts most don't get to see. It's even better that she's not trying to put on a show. She doesn't even know that I own The Edward Corporation yet. Maybe she won't care.

The large window covering half a wall in the bathroom lets in a good amount of light, but I still light a few more candles I left in the bathroom for guests to enjoy a dark bath, so I can see before I climb into the shower and quickly wash off the sweat. After cleaning everything, I flip the water off, and wrap one of the fluffy white towels I purchased for guests around my waist. I glance around the bathroom and realize I forgot to grab extra clothes before I came in here. I groan to myself. I keep a duffel bag of extra clothing in the front coat closet in case I decide to pop in for a night, but in my haste to get clean and eat it slipped my mind.

I reach for the doorknob, square my shoulders, and prepare myself for the show.

# CHAPTER 14

## Alexandra

I HEAR the click of the door from down the hall while I'm moving the plates of eggs, bacon, and pancakes to the small two-person table. "Oh good. You're done. The food is ready." I look up when I hear James's feet padding towards the kitchen.

*Mistake. Holy fuck.*

James is walking towards me with a towel secured low on his hips, water droplets still littering his muscular chest. The spatula in my hand slips from my fingers and clangs to the floor, but I can't look away. His ab muscles form the perfect V where the towel is a breath away from putting on a real show.

"I forgot to grab clothes from the closet." His amused tone has my eyes finally snapping to his face. My face heats like I was slapped with a hot frying pan.

"Ah, right. Well ... the food is ready," I say again and

spin away from him. I quickly collect the spatula from the floor, and take it to the sink to wash it while I reset my brain after it was on the verge of short-circuiting.

James grabs the hand holding the spatula and I almost jump out of my skin. He spins me into his wet chest, and my heart stalls. He trails his other hand up my arm, slowly making his way to my face to brush a loose strand of hair behind my ear. "I like seeing you flustered. I think it's my new favorite."

I can't take my eyes off his mouth. "Your new favorite what?"

His mouth tilts up as he trails his finger across my cheek, down my neck, and stops on my chest. "My favorite shade of red." His hand doesn't move from the center of my chest, hovering right above my breasts. My brain is turning to mush. I honestly have no idea what to say or do. I'm so out of my element.

I step towards the table, stumbling over my own feet. *Dammit.*

James steadies me before smirking again and stalking towards the front coat closet like he didn't just turn my world upside-down. I glance out the corner of my eye, watching as he unzips a bag he pulled from the closet and tosses various clothing onto the bench by the front door, then puts the bag back in the closet. He makes a small stack and cradles it in one hand while he carries a hoodie in the other. Walking up to me, he sets his clothes on the chair across from where I'm still awkwardly standing. He takes the hoodie in his hands and unzips it before sliding it around my shoulders. He nods to himself as if this were his plan all along, picks up his clothing, and walks back towards the bedroom.

I gaze at the sweater and catch his scent. *Ugh. I'm not strong enough for this.*

I slide my arms into the hoodie. It goes down to my thighs and feels like a warm hug. I hum to myself. *How'd he know this was what I really needed?*

I fold myself onto the chair closest to me, fully content now that I have a cozy sweater that smells like pine needles and a hint of cologne. *I should have snuck sweats in my bag when Ashlyn wasn't looking.* I guess this is better. I wouldn't have been able to smell James if I did that. That woman is an evil genius, even if she had no clue this would happen. I chuckle to myself. She's going to die when she finds out.

"What's so funny?" James asks as he walks back down the hallway while pulling a shirt over his body. I catch another glimpse of those abs and *almost* forget what was happening.

"Oh, just how Ash is going to love that this happened." I pick up my fork for something to distract me as James slides into the chair across from me and starts dishing up his food.

He smirks. "I'm sure she will have the same reaction as Ryder when he finds out." He shakes his head. "He's insufferable, but..." James lets his shoulders drop and his eyes soften as calmness radiates off of him. "He's family, along with Alester. They're all I have left."

I rub my socked foot against his leg under the table. "They're lucky to have you." Before things can get heavy for him again, I add, "Plus, now you have me, and I come with Ashlyn, who can keep Ryder busy for you." We both laugh before finally eating breakfast.

I try to casually glance at James, but every time I do, he's looking right at me. *Ugh. I can feel my annoying face heating again.* I wish he'd stop looking at me for a second, so I can blatantly stare at him. If I were braver, I would just suffer the eye contact, but I'm not. I decide to shift the conversation again instead. "I forgot to ask. What do you and your cousins do for work? Specifically."

"We work for a marketing firm. They want to expand to a new location, so we proposed Shadowbrook as an option." He shrugs. "We wanted to be closer to our family."

"What company?" I ask. I saw the name of the company at the club, but I doubt he noticed. I hadn't heard of them expanding to another new location, much less the midwest, and I make sure to keep tabs on all of the marketing firms new opportunities in this area. It must be under lock and key until the big announcement. *Interesting.*

He leans back, watching me. He bites the side of his lip before he answers. "The Edward Corporation."

He blinks like he didn't just drop a huge bomb. The Edward Corporation is a prestigious marketing firm known to produce the best work and the happiest employees. If someone gets hired there, they always retire with them. "You work for The Edward Corporation." I whistle. "No wonder you have everything you do. They're the largest firm to pop out of nowhere. They've been taking over large sections in marketing from coast to coast."

My mind is spinning in overdrive. Maybe he could refer me to his boss, just to get my foot in the door. I mull my lip. No, I don't want to ask him for help because then it feels like this is a transaction, and I really don't want that to happen. I'm sure he gets requests like that all the time. But maybe I could at least add it to my resume that I know the cousins. Then it wouldn't feel like I'm using the man I'm growing to like more and more.

James waves his hand in front of my face. I pull myself out of my hyper anxiety reel. "I said, you've heard of our company?"

I clear my throat and put on my nonchalant face. "Well, yes. Obviously. Everyone has heard of The Edward Corporation. It's legendary in the marketing world." I get up and start bringing dishes to the sink. "That sounds like a cool place to work. My bosses were always terrified of it, anyways."

He chuckles and helps with the dishes.

"Yeah, it's been a really great opportunity." He

follows me to the small sink as we stack empty dishes for washing. Then he gives me a pointed look. "You should get back to painting. It's why you came here, after all."

"But I can clean..." I start.

"No no no. I'm grown. I can handle the dishes, and then I need to bring more wood to the cabin and check on things outside, so I'll be out of your hair for a while." He starts washing, not bothering to look back.

I'm honestly so conflicted. I've never had a man wash my dishes before, but it's kind of nice. After watching for a few seconds, I realize he's right. I need to get to work or I'm never going to land a design job like I want to.

I go to the bedroom and look through my limited clothing for something to paint in today. I can't get paint on his sweater, that will have to be my evening wear. I fold the sweater and place it on the dresser, opting for a black silk set. The shorts and crop T-shirt are lined with lace. It's a good thing James is able to keep the living room warm with the fire, or I'd be a popsicle already.

I glance in the mirror hanging by the door. I take in my hair. It's a little wavy from sleeping and frizzy in places, so I smooth it down and in place as much as possible without getting it wet.

I shrug at my reflection. "Time to get to work or you'll be homeless," I tell myself. It's not fully true. I could move in with my mom, but that would be a nightmare. Maybe Jaz or Ash would let me crash at their place. *No. I will make this work. I will get a job with my work.*

I point at myself in the mirror and walk out of the room straight to my easel.

I can feel him watching me, silently. I'm not sure when he came in from collecting more firewood. I have been so deep in this painting I'm not even sure how much time has gone by. I set my brush on the stool holding my supplies and stretch.

His steps are hesitant at first, then I feel his hands kneading the knots out of my neck. "You are more talented than you realize," he whispers as he places a kiss below my ear. Tingles race through my body, ready for more.

"Mmm." I lean into him, closing my eyes.

He lightly grips my chin, tilting it towards his mouth. "I'm serious. I—"

I capture his mouth with mine. I've never been able to take compliments. Not since my mom told me I would never amount to anything by following my dreams. Anytime I had a piece in an art show, she'd tell me she didn't have the time to see it, and Dad just followed her lead. But you bet your ass we were there for every event my little sister did. It didn't matter if she was just trying something new or had been to a game every week. We couldn't miss those. Now mom is busy throwing herself into every event imaginable, while Dad is off exploring new cities and starting a new family for all we know. I shouldn't care, but there's always a small part of me that does.

I push the thoughts to the back of my mind into their neat little box I keep them locked away in and come back to the present. Slipping my fingers through James's hair, I pull him closer, deepening the kiss and causing a growl to rumble up his throat. His hands slide down my back and over by bare cheeks where my shorts have ridden up, and he uses his leverage to lift me against his hard body. I can feel his length pressing against my center. I grind against him.

James pulls his lips from mine, and I open my mouth to protest. "I need to be inside you," he whispers into my hair. My heart beats faster in anticipation. He looks up into my eyes, waiting.

I bite my lip with a smirk. "God, yes."

"There's a problem though."

I hold in a whine. "What?"

"I don't have any protection with me." He tries to step back, but I stop him.

It's as if another person has taken me over because I'm never this bold. "I'm on the pill. Are you clean?"

He pauses. "Yes, I was checked after my ex, and I haven't been with anyone else since."

"Perfect." I grind against him again removing all hesitation.

He chuckles. "You'll be saying that again soon," he says as he brings me over to the kitchen table and lays me across it, settling my heels on his shoulders. I watch as he slowly slides his hands up my legs, his mouth leaving kisses and bites right behind his hands on his way up to the hem of my shorts. I'm trying not to squirm off the table as his mouth hovers on my center, the hot air of his breath making my body weep for him. James places the smallest amount of pressure against my wound-up ball of nerves, sending my eyes to the back of my head.

*Fuck*.

My whole body shivers involuntarily at the contact. He hooks his fingers around my waistband and drags my shorts ever so slowly down my body. I don't dare move or breathe, afraid he might stop at any moment. I've been anticipating his hands on me again since the moment he saved me in the club. Being here now doesn't even come close to the nights I've imagined my own hands as his. Even with his torturous pace, it's so much better than I could have ever dreamed. But I'm like a feral beast at this point and want nothing more than to forget these past few months ever happened.

His hands slide back up my thighs, slowly. His calluses scrape against my smooth skin, giving me at least some sort of friction. I wiggle on the table, silently begging him to give me the release I desperately need.

James moves one hand to rest on my lower stomach. "Patience. I've waited this long for you. I'm going to take my time." He smiles at me as I whimper under his intense gaze raking over every inch of my body. He continues to hold me in place as he slides one of the chairs in between my spread legs and sits. With one hand holding me down, the other glides back up my thigh, pressing my legs further apart in front of him. The only thing keeping me from being laid bare for him is my tiny lace thong that barely covers anything.

James caresses the edge of my panties leaving me breathless. His thumb slides under the seam of lace, caressing my tightly wound bundle of nerves. My hips jump towards him, but his other hand holds me in place. "Don't worry, baby. I'll take care of you."

My head falls back on the table as a moan floats up my throat. His thumb is like an expert on my body. I know how insane that sounds given we barely know each other. I can't with this man.

He moves the thin material to the side as his thumb continues making slow circles. Then I feel his tongue flick up my center. "Oh my God," I say.

He hums in response but keeps his pace slow and steady, driving me crazy. I'm aching with need, and this climb is showing me how impatient I truly am.

I slide my fingers through his hair, pulling him closer, showing him I want it rougher. He pushes into me with a flick upward then nips at my sensitive center with his teeth.

"Holy fuck!" I throw my head back further, seeing stars, my back arching off the table. He flicks his tongue in circles to soothe the ache before nipping at me again. The mixture of pleasure and pain has me seeing spots. My body shakes from the most intense orgasm of my life.

I grip the table, my nails digging in as I try to catch my breath. I can't function. My entire body is on hyper sensitivity.

James laps up my orgasm, humming the entire time as my body jerks in response to every light touch of his tongue. He does one final swipe and stands slowly, still holding me to the table, and slides his thumb across my bottom lip. My eyes lock onto his as I take his thumb into my mouth, sucking and swirling my tongue around it.

He groans. "I could watch this all day, but don't worry, we will have time for that later. Right now, I'm going to bury myself so deep inside you, you'll forget any other man before me."

I release his thumb with a pop of my lips and smirk before he grabs my ass and slides me to the edge of the table. I yelp at the sudden movement, but now I'm the one who's hungry, watching as he slides his pants off in one smooth motion, his cock springing free.

James prowls back between my legs and looks down. "You're beautiful." He slides his hands up to my hips. "Hold on." I reach out to the sides of the table and wrap my fingers around the curved edges. "Good girl," he says before burying himself inside of me in one thrust.

I gasp and James pauses as he waits for me to adjust to his size. I rotate my hips and wiggle under him. He takes the opportunity to withdraw out and slam back home, again and again. My next orgasm is building when he reaches between us and rubs my clit with his thumb while his other hand lightly grips my throat to hold me in place while he picks up his pace. I grip the edges of the table harder to keep myself from bursting into tiny particles of light, but it's no use. He's an expert at stimulating my body.

"Let me feel you come, Alex."

That's all it takes. The rumble of his voice, the pressure of his fingers, and his delicious cock thrusting into me.

"Fuck!" I arch my body towards James, and he cradles my head as he continues pumping into me, dragging out my orgasm before I feel him tense and spill into me.

"You are perfection." James whispers into my hair, rubbing circles on my shoulder. "I could stay in this moment forever."

All I can do is nod because my body has turned into Jell-o. He slowly withdraws then picks me up and carries me to the bed in front of the fireplace. He gently sets me down before going into the kitchen. He returns a moment later with a warm washcloth and kneels between my legs again. He gently wipes the cloth up my leg to my center.

"You don't need to do that," I say.

He looks up at me while he continues his path. "I want to. I like taking care of you," he says with no room for argument. His hands are slow and soothing as he cleans up our mess.

I want to melt into a puddle or squeal with delight, but both options feel awkward to do with an audience. I cover my eyes and try to hide my stupid smile.

# CHAPTER 15
## James

I'M A GONER. Now that I've had Alex, she's all I want. I don't want this to end here, so I just have to prove to her that this isn't temporary. I have no idea how I'm going to do that, but I'll think of something. I have to.

I slide my sweatpants on, not bothering to clean myself. I like the idea of her staying on me. "I'm going to make us some food," I call over my shoulder as I make my way to the small kitchen, grabbing a pot to start boiling water.

"I can help," Alex calls from the bed, but I shake my head.

"Absolutely not. You relax. Enjoy the fire. It'll be done shortly." I glance back to her painting sitting in the middle of the room and get struck again at how good it is. She isn't done yet, but I can see where she's going. She's painted this place. A view of the cabin from outside, the trees surrounding it with snow everywhere. Large windows lit from within by the fireplace, the glow reflecting off the snow outside.

*My dad would have loved it, just like he loved this place.*

I pour the pasta into the boiling water and stir as I think. *This is what our new chapter needs. The heart and emotion radiating from that simple painting of a cabin in the woods. It's inviting. It brings back memories, for me at least, of my dad and how happy he was here. It feels like home looking at it, and if Alex can do that with a simple cabin, I can't imagine what she could do with the companies we work with.*

Once the power is back and my phone is charged, I need to send a photo to Ryder and Alester and see if I'm crazy, or if she's the artist we need on our team. I'm usually not wrong with these types of decisions, but we are a partnership and I value their opinion in everything we do.

I glance at Alex and watch as she twirls her long brown hair around her fingers while sketching in her notebook. She hasn't stopped painting or drawing since she got here, unless she's eating or sleeping. It's inspiring to watch her creativity unfold. My dad always said this place was magical, but now I can truly see it at work. I pull out some pre-marinated chicken breasts from the fridge and throw them in a pan to cook. This makeshift chicken parm will have to do for an early dinner.

I open the vent for the external exhaust, so the fumes

have somewhere to go then I pull out fixings to throw together a small salad. When the chicken and pasta are done, I dish it onto two plates and sprinkle a healthy amount of parmesan cheese over it before setting it next to the salads.

Alex is lying on her stomach scratching away at her sketchbook when I crawl across the bed and start kissing up her back towards her shoulder. She shifts to look at me, so I place a final kiss on her lips. "Dinner is ready."

"Mmmm." She hums and rolls over, lacing her arms around my neck and pulling me back to her mouth. "I think I'd rather have dessert first."

*Fuck.* She crashes her lips to mine, and I can't bring myself to deny anything she wants from me. I roll to my back, pulling her on top of me, so she can show me exactly how she likes it. We're slow to explore each other. I slide my hands up her stomach, lightly brushing my thumbs under her breasts. She shivers then starts leaving a trail of kisses down my jaw then my neck, and down my chest towards my sweat pants.

"Alex." I warn her, but she ignores me and continues her pursuit. She slides my pants down, allowing me to spring free. I'm already hard for her again. I can't help it when she looks this edible. I watch her lick her lips as she stares at me, and that alone is almost my demise. I groan, wanting to give myself a chance by not watching, but knowing I'd be pissed if I missed a second of learning everything about Alex.

She takes her time, wrapping one hand around my

shaft, while the other cups my balls rolling them gently. "Baby," I say. Her eyes lock on mine. "I don't mean to rush you, but if you don't do something soon, I'm not going to be able to control myself."

The smile that covers her face is like something of a villain about to lay out their evil plans. She doesn't say anything as she slowly leans towards me and takes just the tip into her mouth. She swirls her tongue around me, and I throw my head back in ecstasy. My hips jerk towards her involuntarily, causing her to take me deeper, but she doesn't stop there. She slides me to the back of her throat and uses her hand to help bridge the gap of how far she can take me before she's backing out and starting again. When she ups her pace I pull out, making her lips pop from the suction.

"What do you think you're doing?" she asks and starts reaching for me again, but I back away.

"If you keep that up, things are going to end very quickly." That wicked smile returns as she crawls towards me like she's on a mission to complete what she started. I'm quick to reach around her, grab her by the hips, and toss her onto the bed on her back. Her gasp is cut off when I'm hovering an inch above her face. "I told you before. I like taking care of you, so there's no way you're getting to do that to completion anytime soon." She growls in protest until I start rubbing the head of my cock against her center and up to her clit before circling back and forth. Her entrance is slick with arousal. I hum with approval. "You enjoy taking me deep in your throat?"

She moans in response.

I stop moving, and she whines. "When I ask you something, you answer. Do you enjoy sucking my cock?"

"Yes," she drags out in a hiss. I reward her by sliding my tip inside, just to pull out again. I tease her a few more times to make sure she's ready before I slam to the hilt. Alex arches her back, grinding against me.

"So needy. Hold on, baby." She digs her fingers into the sheets. "Good girl," I praise. I pound into her, over and over as she cries out my name, and I swear I never want any other woman to say my name after hearing Alex scream it through the cabin.

I feel her orgasm getting closer as she clenches around me, so I stop. Her head whips towards me in confusion. "You don't come until I tell you." She opens her mouth to argue, but I'm quick to interrupt. "We're going together," I reassure her. I wait for her to agree before I kiss her sweet mouth.

I continue traveling down her neck and make my way to her perked breast, rolling my tongue around the peak before lightly blowing on it. Her answering shiver urges me to the other one to do the same.

"James, if you don't start moving, I'm going to flip your ass over." The sass has my dick twitching in response, then I'm sliding slowly again. She scrunches her face in annoyance, and I bite back a chuckle. "I swear to—" I slam deep on the next thrust, silencing her. I pick up my pace as she arches off the bed again, happy with my movements.

When I'm close, I reach between us. "Now, Alex." I pinch her ball of nerves, sending her over the edge.

"Oh my god." She clenches around me as her orgasm rocks through her body, and it sends me over the edge. The pulsing of her muscles around my cock has me spilling inside her. I continue to slowly glide in and out until we both can't take it anymore.

I close my eyes as I lay next to her, catching my breath. I feel her nails grazing my chest, then her head curling into the crook of my arm, snuggling in.

I SNUGGLE CLOSE TO JAMES, his cedar scent curling over me. I've never felt this content. I feel so damn comfortable. It's like I finally woke up and came home. That's crazy, I know. I was just in a relationship, even if it turned out to be complete trash, but it feels like a lifetime ago when I'm with James. It's almost like it never happened because now I'm here. I don't want to be that stupid girl who falls for another guy right after a breakup, but...

I look up at his handsome face. I watch the shadows dance across, accentuating his jaw-line. The logs crackling next to us echo in the silence. I follow the shadows to his eyes, the gold within the green shining brighter in the firelight. The way he's looking at me as his lips slowly pull into a smile. *Fuck.*

"What are you thinking about?" His husky whisper

sends shivers down my spine, like an aged bottle of whiskey.

I burrow my head back into his chest to hide from him. "Things I shouldn't."

I feel him shift away from me before he tilts my chin up to look at him, and I want to melt into a girly puddle. "Don't do that." He looks at me like he can see through me to my hopes and dreams, making me want to pull away again. "Don't hide from me. I want to know everything about you. All of your thoughts. I told you we are inevitable. It doesn't matter how it happened, or why. You're mine now." James kisses my lips softly before standing and pulling me after him.

"Where are you taking me now?" I ask as I trip over the blankets, but before I can catch myself, he scoops me into his arms, making me yelp.

His muscular arms are wrapped around me, cradling me to his chest. "I'm making us a bath since we are both a bit dirty." He wiggles his eyebrows at me.

When we enter the bathroom, it's freezing from being so far from the fireplace with the power still off. James sets me on my feet, so he can turn on the water to the claw tub. When the temperature is to his liking he starts adding oils, salts, and bubbles to the water before waving me over to climb in.

I hiss at the heat, but I also love the burn as I slowly lower myself into the still-filling tub. James steps in behind me, sliding his legs to either side and pulling me to his chest. I watch the muscles in his arms flex as he reaches over to the tray holding soaps and oils. He grabs a loofa and lathers a lavender-scented soap on it before he slowly rubs it across each of my arms, to my chest. I close my eyes and lean my head against his hard chest letting him clean me. It feels so nice to be taken care of.

"Tell me your future plans," he says as he starts on my legs.

"Hmm...well, this is embarrassing." I laugh and roll towards him. I settle on the opposite side, so I can look at him.

He starts sliding the loofa up my leg again. "Why would your future be embarrassing?"

I want to hide my face, but I know he will scold me for it. He seems to dislike me hiding from him. "Because you're obviously successful at such a young age, and I'm ... well ... not."

I watch his mouth twitch into a frown. "Don't compare yourself to me. There are a lot of things in my life that didn't go as planned. Everyone's path is different. We aren't meant to succeed or fail at the same time. Everything happens for a reason at the time it's needed to." He looks down at the loofa. "Sometimes I have to remind myself of that too."

I reach for his hand. "Hey, I'm sorry. I know you've been through a lot with your dad. I hope you'll tell me more about him someday." I huff out a breath, pulling on my invisible big-girl pants, so I can rip the whole Band-Aid of my life off. "I recently quit my job without a plan. Well ... I have a plan *now*. *It*'s just not a sure thing. I came here to paint, to create more work for my portfolio, so that I can hopefully get a job in design when I go back home," I spit out as fast as possible.

His eyes light up, like a spark just ignited behind them, but he hides it as quickly as it appeared. "Why is that embarrassing? You're chasing your dreams." He pulls on my hand. "Get over here. I'm proud of you. You'll find the place you're meant to be. I'm sure of it." I slide across the tub back into his arms, and it's the most perfect place I've ever been.

"If I fail, I will have to move in with my mom. And *that* will be the most embarrassing thing in my life."

His chuckle shakes my entire body. "I won't let that happen. You're mine now. You can move in with me. I just got a new apartment near your building, remember?"

I smack his chest. "Yeah, yeah. I remember. Are you sure you'll have enough room in your bachelor pad apartment?" I have no idea how big his place is, but I'm sure it's bigger than my tiny apartment.

"Oh, I've got room. Trust me." When I look at him with confusion, he just winks at me. "Now, get back in position, I need to wash your hair and finish cleaning this gorgeous body of yours."

"Shit, okay." I laugh and spin so my back is against his chest. His laugh ringing out with mine makes my heart feel light and fluffy.

"Sit forward so I can wash your hair first," James instructs, so I do as I'm told and angle my head back.

He pours water over my head with careful precision before he pumps shampoo into his palm, rubs both hands together, then starts lathering my scalp, slowly massaging the soap through my strands. It feels like heaven, and I *almost* let a moan slip. When he rinses the soap out, he slowly trails his fingers down my back giving me goosebumps even in the scalding water.

James fills a palm with conditioner before threading it carefully through the ends of my hair. He's ruining me for anyone else in the world with this treatment, and I think he knows it.

He gently pulls me back against him when he's done with my hair. He re-lathers the loofa and starts on my stomach, swirling in slow circles. Every so often he dips lower, and I rub my legs together in anticipation. James hooks his left leg over mine, pinning it in place while his hand travels between my legs. The loofa glides against my center, making me whimper. It's barely any friction, just a tease.

I bite my lip as I try to stay still. I can feel his heart beat speeding up against my back. After a few more strokes with the fluffy material, he tosses it to the side and slides his fingers across me, circling my clit. I throw my head back against him, arching my back, and pressing further into his hand.

"Needy. And all mine," he whispers into my ear, making me break into a million pieces. He speeds up until I'm coming undone.

I push away from him, so I can turn around to face

him, and place my knees on either side as I hover above him. He's ready for me, and it's all I want as I slowly ease myself onto him.

His answering hiss is all the encouragement I need before I start moving up and down. The soreness between my legs just makes the pleasure more intense. His rough palm slides up my body to my breast. I drop my head back in ecstasy when he rolls the nub between his fingers.

James makes me feel more alive than I have in years. It's addicting.

After draining the tub and cleaning off *again*, we drag ourselves back into the warm living room. I grab a loose T-shirt that hangs off one shoulder and navy lace panties before heading back to my stool. My background with scattered trees is dry, so I squeeze the paint I need for the cabin and more layering for the trees onto my dish. Opening my notebook, I take in the color combinations I wanted to try for this layer. When I blend a new combination, I reach over and place a streak, scribbling the ratio, so I can recreate it later.

The oven beeps, and I glance up confused as James pulls up a chair next to me.

He holds a fork in front of my mouth. "I'm going to feed you while you paint, so this chicken parm doesn't go to waste."

I chuckle but open my mouth for him. He slowly slides it between my lips as I close around the fork. *God damn, why is he good in the kitchen too? Is this a joke?*

"Keep painting," he says as he watches me and cuts another bite.

I smirk, and dip my brush in paint, then slide it across the canvas starting on the cabin. Every time I swallow, James is there with another bite until the plate is empty.

"Good girl," he says, then kisses the top of my head. He takes the dishes to the sink, then makes his way to the bed. He's propped up against pillows on the mattress, writing in a notebook.

"What are you doing down there?" I ask. I haven't seen him writing in a notebook the entire time I've been here.

He glances up after he finishes what he's doing. "Work. I have a lot of ... new things happening with this location, so I wanted to get ahead for when I can get back to the office."

I'd really love to dig more into his time with The

Edward Corporation. It's such a dream job, but it is obviously way out of my league. I'll have to see if they're hiring any entry-level positions for this new location. I bite my lip, thinking, as I dip my brush and keep painting.

I swipe my brush across the canvas, and the lights start to flicker then buzz to life. I glance up in shock then back to James.

He jumps off the mattress. "I'll go check the radio in the shed to see what they have to say about the storm." He slides his boots and jacket on before slipping out the front door.

I go back to adding all the details to my canvas while I wait.

I hear his steps outside the door and the telltale tapping of his boots before the door swings open. "They're working on the main roads, but it will take time before they can get to residential streets. I think the power should stay on now." He kicks off his boots before going to his briefcase and pulling out his phone and charger. "I'm going to plug mine in. Do you want me to get yours while you work?"

I'm almost stunned he asked, but then I remember he keeps telling me that he enjoys taking care of me. "Yes, please. It should be on the nightstand in the bedroom." I continue working as he moves through the cabin to plug in our phones, his laptop, and the other appliances. I'm vaguely aware that our time in our little oasis is coming to an end, but I don't want to think about it. I know I told myself that maybe this could just be a fun weekend, but now after everything, I don't think I'm capable of a just-for-fun relationship.

I feel James press his hard chest against my back before his arms wrap around my middle, pulling me close. His lips press to my neck.

"This is amazing. I can't even fathom how you accomplished getting all the light to reflect off the snow from the cabin. My dad would have loved to see this."

My heart melts hearing him speak of his dad as if he would have brought me home to meet him. I look at the painting again. It's just a rough concept right now with outlines and small amounts of lighting, but he said he grew up coming here so he can tell where my ideas are heading. If he likes it this much at the beginning stage, I'm sure he will love it even more when it's finished.

"I'm going to draft more while you paint." I smile as I watch him start writing again.

It's getting late, but I really want to finish as many layers as I can, so I can finish it completely tomorrow.

# CHAPTER 17
## James

I ROLL over and look out the window, but it's still dark. I try to figure out what woke me from my blissful sleep. I look around the room, just the glow of the fireplace lighting the area, when the buzzing of my phone flashing on the counter catches my attention. *Wow, I really didn't miss hearing that noise all weekend.*

I glance at Alex, but she's still safely dreaming. Her hair is sprawled across the pillow, and her face is scrunched like she's in an argument with someone in her dream. I reach over and rub my thumb over her forehead, and she instantly relaxes and curls further into her pillow. I bite my lip to keep from laughing out loud and slowly climb from the bed, making my way to my phone. I pick it up and scroll through the notifications pouring through. Twenty missed calls from Ryder, five from Alester, hundreds of emails and texts. I slide boots and a coat on before gently closing the front door when my phone starts ringing again.

"Ryder, what's happening? I've only been off the grid for a few days," I whisper-snap at him.

"Holy shit! He answered! Get in here now! Okay. You're on speakerphone with me and Alester." Ryder is in a hyper panic.

"Ryder, focus. What is it?" I roll my eyes as I pace the front porch. The snow is done falling and everything is still. Quiet seeps from all around as the forest sleeps.

"Shit. Yeah, okay. Well, from what Alester can see, a man is trying to poach Family Farms to go to our competitors, Collins and Sons." Ryder is breathing heavily, like he's been running laps around the office while ringing my phone over and over.

My stomach drops. *This can't be happening. I thought things were finally looking up. Now this?*

"James, are you there? Hello? We are trying to find out everything we can, but we need you here. This is your company, and our most important account. They know you best after everything, and they are going to need to see your face to save this."

Alester grunts his agreement.

My mind is turning to static. "Alester, what's happening from your end."

It's silent, then Alester's voice gets close to the speaker. "I noticed some background noise coming through in my programming. I wanted to wait to see what would happen before I told you. I put a flag on the movement. Someone not as tech savvy was trying to dig through our open accounts. I have everything important under lockdown, only public knowledge is accessible as a sort of mouse trap."

"Okay, just get to the point," I huff.

"Right. Right. Okay, well, that's how I caught him. He was digging through those files, then I traced it to a call to our public partnerships and found him setting up a meeting with Family Farms. Someone named Taylor. I'm getting more information on him as we speak. My bots are tracking him and pulling his history."

"Okay..."

I heard him, but it's like I'm under water. My mind is racing back to the hospital. To dad.

*Dad is propped up in his hospital bed. Machines are hooked to his finger and arm, and an IV is stuck in his other arm. His skin is ashen, voice hoarse, as I sit with him, and we go over my college presentation to pass the time. I look back at my notebook. "So, we have to come up with a business proposal for class to pitch and prove it's a doable concept."*

*Dad nods for me to continue. His wheels are turning.*

*"Ryder and I are going over an idea for a marketing company that does full advertisement for emerging and current companies. We would approach them, come up with mockups created by artists, and bring those concepts to other companies that align with their brands to help them bridge the gap. Basically, we do the heavy lifting, so the companies can focus on their day-to-day work."*

*Dad coughs into his hospital gown. A trail of blood smears his sleeve. "That sounds like a great idea, bud. But which company would you start with first?" He coughs again, and this time I try not to look at the blood coming out. Time is fleeting.*

*"Well, it's just for class, Dad. I don't think we need to come up with a legit company." I frown at my notebook, thinking. Bouncing my pen up and down.*

*"Son, we both know once you get an idea, you don't tend to let it..." He coughs again, so I get up and bring the box of tissues closer and fill a cup with water. He wipes his mouth and takes a drink before settling back against the pillows. "Thank you. You don't tend to let ideas go." He pauses and takes another sip of water. "What about Family Farms? They're a small company, not well known, and they're good people. They could use the help getting their name out there."*

*Now my wheels are turning quickly. I'm going to need to bring Alester into this. He's the computer guy and can set up websites to reach more people digitally. Maybe we can get a design student to do our first mockup, for practice. I'm going to have to set up a meeting, maybe Ryder can start reaching out to designers while I do that.*

*"Son?" Dad reaches over and pats my leg.*

*My head snaps up to meet his eyes. They're getting more yellow and glazed over as the cancer spreads through his body and takes over everything. "Yeah, Dad. Just thinking. I'll reach out to them and set up a meeting." I jot down some notes in my book for everything spinning in my head.*

*His weak smile barely reaches his eyes nowadays, as he looks at me. "You're going to do great things, my boy. I'm so proud of you."*

"JAMES! Hello? Are you coming or what?" Ryder screams into the phone. I can hear Alester in the background telling him to calm the fuck down.

"I'm coming. I just have to move some snow first." I click off the line before Ryder can start up again, and quickly get to work.

I will not lose Family Farms. I don't care how small they are. They are endlessly tied to my dad, and I can't lose that after I've already lost *him*.

I rub my hands over my face. I hate that I have to leave the cabin. Alex is everything and it felt like she was finally seeing our possibilities, but I also can't lose this part of my dad. I just hope she will understand why I had to leave so quickly. I don't even remember much of moving the snow or getting in my truck and peeling down the driveway. How I didn't get stuck on the gravel drive is a surprise to me. The tree coverage that I haven't trimmed in a while probably helped with the snow buildup, but I just hit the gas and went.

The entire drive back is a blur, but I'm in the parking lot of Edward Corporation now. I wish I was smart enough to have gotten Alex's number at this point, but I guess I can always have Alester track her down, if I don't find her first.

I kick open the door to my truck and make my way into the building. It's time to get to work.

PART
Two

# CHAPTER 18

## James

I MAKE my way into my building, bypassing security. Thomas sits at his desk in the front lobby, it's just somewhere for him to relax and do whatever else he likes to do while he waits for us to need him. He tries to get my attention, but I'm not in the right mindset to interact with anyone but my cousins.

I rush to the elevator and stab the button for the top floor. Impatiently, I tap my foot on the slick floor as the elevator slowly ascends up the thirteen floors. Half of this building is still sitting empty as we hire and remodel different floors for what will work for our company, but still, this building is too big for what we need. I'll either need to expand operations or rent out some of the floors. The latter makes my skin crawl, but if they're companies I work with that might need a drop in space, that I could work with. I pull out my phone to send an email to Stacy about my idea and to draft some proposals, even in a crisis ideas can't be ignored.

Stacy stands when the elevator doors open, and I step out onto our floor. I wave for her to sit. "Later, Stace." She nods and goes back to working on her computer. She's used to the three of us in crisis mode, and with the way Ryder sounded on the phone, I'd guess she's been dealing with it the entire time I've been gone.

I slam my office door closed after I walk through it.

Ryder and Alester have been waiting in here since we got off the phone hours ago, I'm sure.

"Tell me where we are?" I throw my coat on the couch in my office and make my way to the desk, powering on the computer. Ryder sits in the chair across from me while Alester leans in the corner of the room with his arms crossed, awaiting a command.

"Why don't you tell me how the cabin was?" Ryder is definitely hiding something trying to change the subject. That was always his tell ever since we were little.

I can't play this game, not with the last part of my dad on the line. The part of the company that he helped create. Yeah, sure I have plenty of money and this won't end us by a long shot, but that's not the point. This is personal. This is a piece of him that I refuse to let go of, no matter what.

"I'm not in the mood. Where are we? Now," I say, glaring at him until he finally drops it.

Alester coughs into his sleeve, throwing a look at Ryder that I choose to ignore. "His name is Taylor McAllister. He was apparently promised a large promotional position if he was successful in securing multiple contracts. So far, I can only see correspondence between him and the two idiot sons of Collins and Sons. Also, he used to date Alexandra Lewis." His body language doesn't change, always the one to deliver facts without emotion. Ryder, on the other hand...

I lean back, pressing my fingers together. "Taylor?" Alester nods. "And *my* Alex?" Alester raises an eyebrow but nods. "Fuck." I spit my words at the ground. *Why in the fuck?*

"We can get the companies to stay. We just need to contact them and make our offer more attractive before they sign any contracts." Alester says.

I crack my neck. "There's only one company I care about. I will talk to them myself, but first I need to figure out why. Why Taylor and why my clients?"

"James, our clients are desirable because of our reputation." Ryder stands. "We don't know how Taylor got through to contact any of them, or why they're giving him the time of day. It doesn't look like he's made any real strides in the marketing world. Just an average nobody. But there's the link to Alex..." He shrugs. His eyes are pleading with me to stay calm, but I don't even know how this happened.

I glare at him. "Yeah, I get it. She was never near my laptop, but I get what you're throwing out there."

I get up and grab my coat again, shouldn't have taken it off in the first place.

"But you did bring it to the cabin?" Ryder asks. "This involves all of us, and we don't want to see you get hurt again. Rebecca did enough damage."

I groan. "There was literally no time for Alex to get into it, crack my password, and forward concealed documents. I'll figure it out. Alex isn't Rebecca, so you can remove that from your brain right now. Leave your phones on. We start making calls first thing in the morning. This has to get fixed."

I head back out the door, trying to calm myself down and reassure myself that there's no way Alex knew. If she did, this weekend wouldn't have happened...right? I can't be getting fucked over again by a woman. No, not Alex. She's nothing like Rebecca, and she was certainly shocked when I told her who I 'work' for. Rebecca...I should have seen the red flags from the beginning.

*Rebecca was at one of our first events to celebrate the new up-and-coming company flourishing in design and marketing, The Edward Corporation. She was dressed in a blue gown, her blonde hair curled to perfection falling down her shoulders, and her black heels clicked all the way to our table.*

*"Congratulations, gentlemen." She leaned over the table, her blue eyes shining as she took me in. I had dropped out of my college program when our company had taken off. I just buried my dad a week ago. Everything was raw.*

*She pulled out the chair next to mine and slid in close. She asked questions about the company and how we got to where we were. I thought she genuinely liked me, but I was also just an idiot college kid who didn't have a clue about the real world. I was coming into big money with big dreams and the grief of watching my dad die. I trusted easily and fell hard.*

*Rebecca was pushing for an engagement ring pretty early in our relationship, wanting to make sure she was at every event we were invited to, and pulled me to take photos with the paparazzi every chance she got. I thought she was proud of our success, but it turned out she just wanted in on the cash and fame.*

*Alester was the one who found the bank statements of her syphoning money from our accounts. She had access to my computer whenever we stayed at my place. Thousands of dollars gone, which at the beginning was a lot. Now, it's nothing. I'm sure I would have kept it going, maybe even married her, had I not caught on. Then she would have had her hands in everything.*

I shake my head. These goddamn memories won't leave me alone. Alex isn't Rebecca. And I'm going to have to prove it to myself.

> James: Pull up Taylor's location and send it to me.

I make my way through the front lobby. Thomas is already waiting with the SUV parked outside the front door. My phone buzzes as I reach the vehicle and slide through the door Thomas has waiting open. I pull my phone out of my pocket and glance at the response from Alester.

Alester: I'll get it. Give me five minutes.

I tap my fingers against the window.

"Where to, James?" Thomas asks. His worried eyes bore into me from the rearview mirror.

"We have to wait for Alester to send us the location. Just go to the Coffee Shop. I haven't eaten anything all day. I'm going to need caffeine to get through this mess."

Thomas takes off at the request. It's only a couple blocks away, so as Thomas orders for us, I pull out my phone to send another message to Alester.

James: I also need Alex's number.

Alester: Are you sure that's a good idea? You could tip off Taylor if they're working together.

James: Are you saying they're working together?

Alester: Obviously not. You can read, can't you?

James: Great, smart ass. I want the number.

Alester: Give me time.

I scoff. I know damn well his software can get phone numbers instantly. He's just trying to delay the inevitable.

Thomas hands me a black coffee before he pulls into a parking spot. I sip the scalding liquid as I wait. Thankfully my phone buzzes a minute later with a text.

> Alester: Here's the link for his address. Don't approach without talking to Ryder about legal implications.

*Yeah, I'm not an idiot.* Time to follow this rat to its hole.

This is ridiculous. I've been sitting outside Taylor's shitty apartment for hours, and he still hasn't bothered to leave yet. At this point, I don't think he will and I should just try again tomorrow.

It's starting to get dark out when I pull my phone out of my pocket. "Let's just head back towards the apartment." Thomas starts the vehicle and pulls out of the apartment parking lot. I shoot a text to Alester, thoroughly irritated.

> James: Number. Now.

Alester: Rude. 567-243-8972

*Finally.* It hasn't even been a full day yet, and I'm itching to get back to Alex. She booked my cabin for an entire week, so I need to figure this shit out. Fast. A week without Alex sounds like torture.

Alester: Don't do anything stupid.

James: Like fall in love?

Alester: I mean…depends if she knows about Taylor or not.

James: Doubtful.

I open a new message. Fully ignoring the new messages pouring in from Alester and a few from Ryder.

James: How's the cabin?

567-243-8972: Who is this?

James: I told you we are inevitable. Don't tell me you can forget about me that fast?

I stare at my phone anticipating the buzzing sensation of the response from Alex. She takes her time, and it almost feels like it's intentional. Especially after getting to know her this weekend.

Alexandra: Hmm. Odd way to show you care by bailing in the middle of the night.

James: Let me make it up to you.

Alexandra: I'm listening…

Okay. I have to make this good. I can't risk losing her now. I need time to think.

James: Tell me when you're home. I have a surprise.

I STEP BACK from my painting, giving it space so I can really take in the full creation. The background of the snow-covered evergreen trees with the moon causing the freshly fallen snow to sparkle. The cabin is the focal point with its log siding and large windows. The fireplace is glowing from within and projecting warmth out the windows. I added small details through the windows, a table with small cocoa cups steaming and fluffy blankets strewn on furniture. I hope I give viewers the feeling of being cozy and warm by the fire while the snow is still outside. I also added a few small details outside in the fresh snow. Small footprints from deer and rabbits. A white rabbit hiding under an evergreen. The highlights from the moon and fire give a small glimpse of the wildlife.

I bite my lip, happy with how it turned out. I could

sit here and add more details for days, but at some point, I have to just let it go and be done.

I pick up my phone and open James's message from last night again. *What kind of surprise does he have planned after leaving in the middle of the night?*

I want to send him another message, but I also want to make him work for this. He's adamant that we are inevitable, so I guess I will see what his actions say.

I make my way down the hall to the bedroom. The small cabin feels so empty without James here. I thought I wanted to disconnect for an entire week, but now ... Now I just want to get back to reality and start applying for jobs. Maybe see what this surprise is all about.

I roll my suitcase out of the closet and open it on the bed. I'm slowly adding my items to the bag when my phone buzzes on the bed next to me.

> James: I can't stop thinking about you. I can't wait to see you again. <3

I touch my fingers to my lips. The ghost of his kiss still lingering as I read his message over and over. Ugh. I'm a lost cause. This man has done something to me that can't be undone.

I throw the rest of my clothes in my bag, double-check the bathroom and closet, and roll my suitcase to the front door. I cleaned the dishes and picked up the living room when I woke up this morning, so there isn't much to do besides take my things outside and lock up. I'm going to miss this cute little cabin, but I'm so excited to photograph my new piece and get my application submitted to marketing agencies in my area. Especially now that I know The Edward Corporation is building a location here.

It was quicker than I thought, but this little oasis gave me everything I needed and more.

It's time to put my life back together.

I pull into my parking stall at the apartment complex and pop my trunk. All of the snow from this weekend has been moved and the roads are clear. It's almost as if the storm never happened, except it's still freezing outside.

I shiver in my giant coat as I make my way around my car. I had to stuff my suitcase in my back seat since my canvas was still a little wet when I loaded it. I'm careful as I take it out, making sure I don't touch any possible wet spots while I carry it up the thirty-two steps to my door. My purse is slung over my shoulder, keys buried. *Dammit. Not again.*

I balance the painting on one hand while I shove the

other deep within my bag, sloshing the contents back and forth until I feel my set of keys. "Fuck yes!" I pull them out slowly, so I don't jostle my entire body and send my hard work flying to the ground. Once the key is safely inserted and the door handle turns, I quickly grab the painting with both hands again, backing into my home. *Thank goodness. Things are finally looking up for me!*

I set the canvas on my spare easel, and take a few photos to scan into my applications. I'll worry about unloading the rest of my car later. Now I have things to do.

I check the quality of the photos on my computer, making slight adjustments so it really shows how amazing the digital version of the canvas can be. My phone dings a few times echoing from the kitchen counter, but I ignore it as I continue uploading documents into my jobs file and filling out multiple applications at once.

BANG. BANG. BANG. The front door rattles as someone's fist continues to hit the wood.

"I'm coming! Go easy on the door," I say as I climb from my desk and make my way to the door before whoever it is can break it off the hinges. The peep hole on my door has been cracked since I moved in, so I don't bother trying to check who it is. I just flip the lock and throw open the door. I flinch, taking in the person on the other side. "What the hell are you doing here?"

"I wanted to see you," Taylor says as he leans on my doorframe.

"You've seen me." I say as I swing the door shut. It bangs on his foot he has shoved in the doorway. He uses his leverage to push the door open and walk in. I pinch the bridge of my nose, trying not to scream. "You need to leave," I say.

"Oh. Come on, Sugar. You know we aren't done." He takes in the new living room furniture, rapping his knuckles on the backrest. "Nice couch."

I roll my eyes, still holding the door open. "No, and don't call me that. We're done and you're done. It's time to leave. And if I didn't make that clear when I threw you out the last time, I never want to see you again."

He continues to ignore me as he paces around my living room taking it all in, looking in every nook and cranny. "Are you seeing someone else already?" he asks.

"I'm not really sure why that's any of your business considering you were already seeing someone else while we were together," I snap.

"Ouch, sugar. I wouldn't call that seeing someone. I was just scratching a need so I wouldn't bother you," he says, eyeing me as if he really believes the bullshit he's spewing at me. "I was being a good boyfriend by letting you focus on your career."

I scoff and laugh because I can't believe someone can be this idiotic. "That's great. I'm so glad you didn't want to bother me. But it's still time for you to go." I walk over to him to shove him out the door, but he grabs my wrist.

Taylor pulls me towards his face, invading my

personal space as I try to yank my arm free. "Just one thing before I let you get back to missing me."

I seethe, feeling like my head is going to explode. "What?" I whisper through clenched teeth. I want to scream as loud as I can. The sound echoes inside of me from holding it in.

He brings his face so close to mine that the smell of his cheap cologne threatens to suffocate me. "I need you to keep distracting your new boy toy, so I can finish my deal. Then you'll never hear from me again."

I whip my head further away from him, but his fingers dig deeper into my wrist keeping me in place. "You're hurting me." He blinks at me but doesn't release his hold. "What are you even talking about? How do you know who I've been with?"

He laughs, but it doesn't sound like the laugh he used when we dated. He sounds deranged, his whole demeanor seems different, or maybe I'm just starting to see the real him. "Oh, I know everything you've been up to. *My* future rides on fucking over your new boyfriend, so I've been keeping close tabs on you. Especially after seeing you at the club. It was the perfect opportunity. You see. You think we are done, but really, you've been helping me even more now that we are on our break."

"We are never getting back together! You were a mistake! What the hell do you want with James? I don't even know what you're talking about." I try to rip my arm free again, but he won't budge.

"Ouch. I could never be a mistake. Don't act dumb

now. You know he's worth billions. His company is taking over in multiple states, with more planned in the future. I just want a piece of the pie to impress my new company, Collins and Sons. That blonde you were so worried about is Collins's granddaughter. She's helping me get a leg up in the company. Your boyfriend has plenty of money, he won't even miss it." He pauses. "Well, he won't miss it *much*, I just need to get these clients to sign off, then I could care less what you do."

I can't even fathom what is happening right now. "James works for The Edward Corporation, he doesn't have billions. Trying to steal clients from another marketing firm is lazy. How is that going to impress Collins and Sons? Did you even do research before concocting this plan?" I yank on my arm and Taylor finally releases me but positions his body in front of the door.

"Tsk, tsk, tsk, Alex. You know I hate when you lie. I know you've been around him and his partners multiple times. I caught you at the club, remember? I watched when they helped you move the couch. I know you've been away with him. What I don't know is why the hell you're back already?" He prowls closer, hate burning in his eyes as he looks down his nose at me.

My heart is racing. I try to glance for a way out, but he has me boxed in. My fight or flight is kicking in, but my body doesn't know how to react, so I freeze. "Why are you doing this?"

He blows out a breath and laughs, backing towards

the center of the room. "Redirecting *again*. Never one to answer questions." Taylor runs his hands across his face. "I need this promotion, and the fastest way to get it is to poach clients. So, if you would've just kept James occupied, then my job would've been done already. You *will* contact him and keep him busy for the week."

The change in his voice and his body language has me on edge. The hair on the back of my neck tingling. I throw my hands in the air. "And if I don't?"

He reaches over, grabs my vase of flowers and launches it towards me. I jump to the side as it slams into the wall next to me, shattering. "You don't want to find out, so figure it the fuck out!" He stomps to the door and storms out. The door slams shut behind him.

I'm shaking as I slide to the floor. I don't know what the hell is going on. Is James more important at his job than he made it seem? Why would Taylor want to target him? My mind is in hyperdrive as my anxiety rolls through my body. The adrenaline coursing through my veins. My phone buzzes on the counter again, so I crawl over to my stools and use them to pull myself up.

Ashlyn: How is the cabin going?

Jaz: The snow here was insane. Are you safe?

I never responded to James's message from this morning, so I pull that open first.

Alexandra: Hey. I'm home. Something happened with Taylor. I need to see you.

His message comes immediately.

James: I'm on my way.

I CAN'T STOP the constant stream of memories flying through my mind even though Alex's message makes me lean towards the side of her not knowing anything.

*Billionaire swindled out of large settlement from ex-fiancé. Sources say she black mailed Mr. Edward, but those claims have not been confirmed.*

*Ex-fiancé backs Mr. Edward into large pay-out to keep quiet about breakup. What was he hiding?*

"We're here, James." I look towards the mirror at the sound of Thomas's voice. Those eyes have seen me through a lot of tough moments. He knows how hard this is for me.

I climb out of the SUV and walk to the stairs of Alex's building. I knock softly on her door. I can hear her feet pad across the floor as she makes her way to me. I need to get her to move into my place as soon as she's willing. This apartment doesn't give her much privacy.

The door slowly cracks open, and I see one dark brown eye peek at me before she swings it all the way open.

"Oh my God. You came." She rushes into my arms and squeezes me.

I wrap my arms around her and walk her backward. "I'm here. It's freezing out, so you need to stay inside." I kick the door closed behind us. "What happened?"

She refuses to look at me while she speed-dumps everything that happened when Taylor came over. By the time she tells me he threw a vase at her, I'm ready to go beat the shit out of him. She takes a breath then tilts her head back to look at me. "Say something."

"I'm going to kill him," I say calmly.

Alex slaps my chest. "Don't you dare. He's not worth it."

I rub a hand down my face. "Well, I'm not going to sit and do nothing. You're getting a new door, so you can actually see who's here."

"You can *not* buy me a new door." She throws her hands on her hips.

I pull her back against my body and slide my hands up her back. "Okay, then you'll come move in with me so I know you're safe."

Alex's eyes bulge like a cartoon character's. "What! How do you make that big of a leap?"

I cup her adorable face in my hands. "You're mine. I

want you safe. There is no large leap." I kiss the tip of her nose. "Mine."

"Okay, cave man." She scrunches her nose at me, but she can't hide her lips pulling up in the corners.

"You like it."

"Maybe," she says as she lays her head on my chest. "What are we going to do?"

I sigh. "We are going to go to my apartment together. Then I will have a bunch of meetings in the morning, while you stay safe." I spin her towards the hallway and give her a tap on the ass. She yelps and glances over her shoulder. "Go pack a bag. With clothing you can wear outside of the bedroom included."

"Ugh. That wasn't my fault!" she says as she pads off to her bedroom.

I pull out my phone and send a group text to Alester and Ryder.

> James: We have a problem. Taylor came after Alex and threatened her.

> Ryder: Fuck.

> Alester: So she's not in on it with him then. We need to have a meeting with Collins and Sons.

> James: I need to go to Family Farms before that.

> Ryder: What about Taylor?

> James: I'll handle him.

Alester: I don't think that's a good idea.

Ryder: Yeahhhh that could end in jail time or a lawsuit.

James: What the fuck am I supposed to do? Let him attack her and get away with it?

Alester: I have a plan, but I can't put it over chat. Talk tomorrow an hour before the meeting.

James: Fine.

I stuff my phone in my pocket just as Alex comes back into the hall holding a small duffle bag. I frown. "Is that going to be enough stuff?"

She rolls her eyes at me then pats my chest when she reaches me. "Don't worry, big guy. *If* I move in, eventually, you'll need a truck to get it all. This is just temporary." She winks and goes to the door.

"That's what you think, babe. You're never going to want to leave once I have you." She stands at the door with her mouth open. I slowly prowl up to her and use the tip of my finger to lift her chin while my other hand slides the bag off her shoulder and onto mine. "I'll take that, love." I wait in the hall for her to lock up then take her hand in mine as we walk out of the building.

Alex squeezes my hand. "I can carry my own bag, you know."

I look down at her cute face. I don't know how I

ever thought she could have anything to do with Taylor. Even if it was brief. "I know you *can*. That's not the point."

"What is the point?" she asks.

I pull open the door to the rear seat of the SUV waiting out front and help her get settled. I grab the seatbelt and drag it slowly across her chest, making sure I lean into her until my mouth is hovering above hers. Her eyes dilate in anticipation.

"I told you. I love taking care of you. I want to do it all." I click the belt into the holder then slide my hand up under her chin and through her hair before I press my lips to hers. Her soft hum vibrates through me as I slip my tongue into her mouth. She melts under my touch as I devour her right in the back seat. I pull back with one last kiss and take in her lust-filled eyes. "We will continue this at my place."

"What—" Her eyes shift to the front seat, finally taking in Thomas, who's staring out the windshield. Red travels up her neck to her cheeks. "Oh my God! I'm so sorry, Thomas."

"Nothing to be sorry for, Ms. Alex."

I chuckle and close her door before I jog around the SUV to the opposite side and slide into the seat next to her.

Alex leans close to my ear. "You're a bad influence."

"You like it." I thread my fingers through hers. Thomas pulls out of the parking lot and heads towards my apartment. Alex rests her head on my shoulder and closes her eyes. I will protect this woman with everything I have.

It doesn't take long before we are pulling into the parking garage attached to my building since it's only a few blocks away from Alex's place. "Thanks, Thomas," I say. "You can head home. We shouldn't need you the rest of the night."

"I'll leave my phone on in case something pops up." Thomas gets out of the vehicle and opens my door.

I pick up Alex's duffle bag, climb out of the SUV, and pat Thomas's shoulder. "What would we do without you?"

Thomas shrugs. "Probably nothing good." He chuckles. "Have a good night and take care of your girl. I'll be a call away if you need me."

"Will do." I open Alex's door and take her hand. "Time to explore your new home." I wink at her. "You can change whatever you want."

Her giggle is music to my ears. "I don't think that's necessary. I barely decorate my own apartment."

A nervous energy travels up my spine as we get to the elevator. I pull out the penthouse key and slide it into the slot so the button will take us all the way up. Alester and Ryder are the only ones with an extra key.

*I should probably make Alex one now too.* Well, that's if she doesn't freak out after seeing my place. My hands are getting clammy. It's like I'm back in grade school, about to ask out a pretty girl. But it's Alex, the girl of my dreams, and me worrying she's going to leave after she sees a glimpse of my real life.

"This is a fancy apartment building. I've never seen an elevator require a key before, but it makes it a lot more secure than my building with no elevator or external lock," she says.

I turn towards her and watch her trail a finger over the gold railing lining the inside. I choose to not say anything as the elevator dings and the doors slide open revealing a small entryway with another door. The marble flooring with gold lines woven throughout are a stark contrast to my black dress shoes and Alex's fuzzy winter boots.

"Wow," she whispers. A bead of sweat drips down my back as I unlock the front door.

"It's just an apartment," I try to reassure her as I swing the door open. She hesitantly steps through the doorway, shedding her coat and shoes, before wandering farther in. Her eyes are wide as she takes in the modern open concept living space. Gleaming black countertops line the kitchen with a white floor throughout with grey accents. I bought a large maroon couch to break up the dull colors and to hide spills when Ryder comes over with food.

I watch Alex wander through the kitchen and into the living room. She stops in front of the projector TV lining an entire wall in front of the couch.

"Say something," I whisper behind her.

The silence is killing me. She spins towards me with a

smirk. "The Edward Corporation must pay really well to set you up in this place."

"It does okay. I didn't want to opt for this building, but Ryder insisted." The relief of her not yelling at me is consuming.

"Wait. Ryder lives with you?" She glances over her shoulder like he's hiding behind her. I can't help but laugh.

"God, no. But he and Alester do live on the next floor down...and he has a key. He sometimes pops in uninvited." She nods, then nearly jumps out of her skin when the front door bangs open.

As if he was summoned, Ryder's voice echoes through the main living area. "Yo! I brought pizza! Let's watch the race." Ryder walks through the entryway towards the living room where we are standing and stops. He's in sweatpants and a sweater, his hair sticking in every direction. "Oh. Didn't know you had company." Ryder shakes off his confusion and continues towards us. "I have plenty of pizza, so don't worry. I'll just squeeze past you to my seat there." I turn to the side, so he doesn't dump the three boxes of firestone pizza he's barely keeping control of and watch as he plants himself in the center of the large sectional. He carefully places each box in their own spot on the table in front of him, then opens them all before taking a slice and settling back.

I run a hand through my hair. "Uh, Ryder. What are you doing here?"

I shoot Alex a sympathetic smile, but she just shrugs. She walks over to the boxes, picks out a slice, and settles in the far-left corner of the couch.

Ryder frowns at me and points at the screen where the dirt bike pre-races are happening. "It's ... race day. You want me to watch it alone?"

I sigh, caving like I always do when it comes to his sad eyes. I walk over to Alex and snuggle in close to her. "Fine. But after the race you're going home." Alex giggles then tries to hide behind her pizza when I look down at her. I bop her on the nose. "What are you giggling at?"

"Even she knows that's ridiculous. We will be having a game night after the race," Ryder says as he stares at the television, avoiding the daggers I'm shooting at him. I finally have Alex in my apartment and he wants to be a giant cock block. "I already texted Alester and told him to bring snacks." He munches on his pizza, completely oblivious, so I launch a pillow at his face. His head rebounds, and he almost drops his slice of pizza. "Dude, not cool." He finally looks at me. "Ew. What's your problem?"

Alex laughs harder. "I think game night sounds fun."

My eyes ping-pong between them. The sound of the front door swinging open locks in my fate.

I lean back and put my arm around Alex. "Fine."

"I brought a couple bags of chips and fresh cookies from the bakery." Alester tosses the snacks next to the pizza then plops down in his spot on the opposite end of the couch. "Hey, Alex. Fancy seeing you here."

"Super fancy," she says before diving for a cookie. "So, this is what you guys do all the time? Couch surf with snacks?"

"Pretty much," I respond before Ryder jumps in.

"Unfortunately. If I want to go out, I can usually drag Alester, but James is an old man already and hates the club." He dodges the next pillow I throw, and it hits Alester.

"Dammit. Ryder, quit being annoying or we are going to make you watch the race by yourself." Alester reprimands before taking a slice of pizza.

Ryder and Alester start taking bets on who's going to win tonight's race while teaching Alex the ins and outs of motocross racing. Through it all, Alex can't stop laughing and I love the sound. Even if Ryder being obnoxious is most of the cause.

I like having them all together. It feels right.

When the races end, it's late and Alex is asleep on my chest. "Alright," I whisper. "No game night. I'm taking her to bed. You'll have to play poker at your place."

Before Ryder and Alester can respond, I scoop Alex into my arms and walk to my bedroom.

As I lay her in the center of my bed, she stirs. "I can play poker. I'm awake." Alex props herself up on her elbows.

"Shh. You can play another night. Tonight, you're mine, and I'm going to enjoy cuddling you again."

"Just cuddling?" She pulls her sweater over her head, so she's just in a white lace bra.

"Alex," I growl in warning.

She slowly slides her yoga pants down her legs. "James."

I stand frozen at the side of the bed. "You need to rest. You've been through a lot."

Alex crawls across the bed towards me in just her underwear. I clench my hands trying not to reach out to her. She slides her hands up my sweater and across my abs. I flex involuntarily, and my resolve is starting to crack. "I think I'll rest after. I'm wide awake now."

She waits. Batting her eyes up at me. "Fuck it." I pull my sweater over my head with one swipe. The grin that takes over her face is electric.

I scoop my arm behind her legs and flip her onto her back. She squeals and giggles, but it quickly turns into a gasp when I drop to my knees and pull her to the edge of my bed. I run my tongue from her ankle to her thigh, nipping and sucking all the way up. I scrape my teeth next to her center, so close but not quite where she wants me. Her hands fly into my hair as a moan escapes her lips.

It's late and I've missed this, so I'm going to take my time. I drag her panties slowly down her body before I make my way back to her. She's ready for me, but I want to devour her like she's my favorite dessert. Slow and torturous. At the first swipe, my sweet Alex is wriggling under my tongue. Her endless moans make me never want to stop.

I can feel her muscles contracting around my fingers with each thrust, and when she finally crests the top I ensure to milk every last drop. I could taste only her for the rest of my life and die a happy man.

Her eyelids are heavy as she tries to reach for me, but I dodge her. "You're exhausted. I'll clean you up then we are going to sleep. End of discussion." I go to my connected bathroom and get a warm washcloth before kneeling between her legs and gently wiping her clean.

"But what about you?" she whispers.

The nervousness flitting across her eyes about breaks me. I tip her chin up and get an inch away from her little nose. "Babe, I'm a grown man. I can wait forever for you if I have to. One night isn't going to hurt me." I kiss her slowly like we have all the time in the world before I lay next to her and pull her naked body flush against mine. I plant one last kiss on her head before I whisper, "Good night, beautiful."

"Good night, James." Her voice is soft, her breathing getting deeper. I think she's asleep, but then I barely hear her mumble, "I think I love you."

"Alex, baby?"

She doesn't respond. She's definitely asleep. This woman has me wrapped around her finger, and I don't think she fully understands it. I slide my phone off the nightstand and type in an order to be delivered in the morning bright and early. Then I send a reminder to Thomas that we need to leave at six in the morning for the meetings to ensure my clients don't go anywhere. I set my alarms, toss the phone back on the nightstand, and wrap my arm back around my girl.

Everything is going to be perfect. It has to be.

A few hours later, I silence my alarm that's buzzing next to me. Alex is so exhausted she doesn't even stir. I carefully untangle my limbs from hers as I slide from the bed. She's mumbling in her sleep again, but I can't make out what she's saying. Her hair is splayed across the pillow. I could stand here all day and watch her sleep, but I have to prep things for when she wakes up later and gets dressed.

I take a speed shower. I have an hour before I told Thomas to be ready.

I make my way to the entry way of my apartment and open the door. On the other side, before the elevator, is everything I ordered. "Perfect." I move it to the kitchen then get to work setting up my girl's surprise.

My phone buzzes in my pocket as I'm closing the door to one of my spare rooms.

Thomas: Out front.

*Shit.* I race through the kitchen and grab my briefcase off the counter before throwing my shoes on. I'm in the elevator within two minutes, but still slightly later than I wanted to be. Good thing I always plan on being early, so I'm never late.

Thomas has the back door open and ready by the time I step out of the building.

The second I'm in, he shuts the door and walks around to the driver's seat. "Good morning, sir. Where to first?"

"Family Farms headquarters. Jake will be up working on the farm already."

Thomas maneuvers the car out onto the road, making his way out of the city. Headquarters is literally Jake's family farm. They raise cattle along with tilling farm land that they've had for generations.

Thomas locks eyes with me in the mirror. "Are you worried, James?" All I can see is fatherly worry.

"Not at all. But it is always good to reach out directly to the people you work with. Remind them that they are more important than the contract they signed. Jake is level-headed. He will be able to see what games Taylor is playing. I just need to make sure he's still confident in us."

It's true. I'm not worried. I have a plan, but Jake took over from his grandparents two years ago. He's young. Level-headed but young, so I need to make sure our deal is still desirable. Thomas doesn't ask any more questions as we make the trek to the farm.

When the SUV crunches across the gravel road, I slide my laptop and notes back into my briefcase. Farmers like to do business differently than city businessmen. It's not about the paper and pen. It's personal. Everything is a conversation and keeping your word with the legal documents coming in last.

Thomas turns down Jake's long driveway, and I scan out the window at the miles of land Jake owns. Thousands of acres for farming and cattle. It's not something an average person gets up and starts. You have to be born into it or have a shit load of money and resources, which isn't common.

Jake spots us from the field and turns his horse in our direction, galloping to the vehicle.

"Stay in the car, Thomas. This shouldn't take long."

Jake isn't the type of person who understands letting a driver open doors for you. I don't really enjoy it either, but Thomas has been a driver forever and likes to stick to the old ways.

I step out of the SUV and wait for Jake to reach me. His black horse is massive the closer they come.

"Whoa." Jake stops the horse then pats his neck before dismounting. "James. It's been a long time. I didn't think we had a meeting scheduled."

"I'm sorry to interrupt. I know you're a busy man. I just wanted to come check in with you."

Jake laughs as he walks the horse to the gate near us and loosely ties him. "Let's take a walk." He turns before making sure I'm following, which I do. We make our way to his main barn where he likes to conduct business. His cowboy boots echo off the ground as he walks. He set up an office out here, so his home can stay private.

I close the door behind us as we make our way to his large conference table. "Coffee?"

"That sounds great. Thanks." I take a seat as he fills two mugs.

He slides a mug to me before sitting in the seat across from me. He places his hat on the table then takes a drink. "I'm assuming this visit is about that Taylor guy."

"We did hear about that, but this visit is more to check in with you. See if you need more from us. We've been doing business with your family since the start of my company, and my first priority is your farm." Jake sits, quietly sipping from his cup, while his dark eyes take in everything I'm not saying. "I'll take care of Taylor. It's my next stop actually. As I'm not convinced the story I'm hearing is true, but if he offered you a better package that is of interest to you, I'd like the opportunity to make a counter offer."

Jake sets his mug down with a chuckle. "Shit, James." He looks up at his rustic ceiling. "You know I don't like dealing with city people. And that Taylor guy. Well, let's just say he didn't get the warm welcome he was looking for." He takes me in, calculating his next words. "I wouldn't mind readjusting our contract though, since you're here."

"I figured you'd enjoy that."

We dive into his business needs. He wants to expand his cattle and get his reach a little further, but given his family was my first contract, I will always keep their rates lower. Which is where Taylor will never be able to compete because any company he works for will never be willing to take as deep of a cut as I do with Family Farms.

"Great. It seems like you'll be ready to dive in when you get your new designer on board," Jake says as he stands. "That timeline should work great for my production too. I'll be moving the cattle to a different field soon, so I'll be busy until that's done."

I get up from my chair and reach out to shake his hand. "Sounds great. I should have some designs sent to you within a couple weeks at most. You can get back to me whenever you're done with your work."

"Perfect." He places his cowboy hat back on his head, and I follow him out of the barn. "I wouldn't worry about Taylor if I were you."

"Why's that?" I ask.

Jake shoves his hands in his jean pockets. The wind is picking up, the temperature unforgiving today. "He isn't grown enough to be making business decisions. He had no idea the farm had changed hands, no knowledge of current prices, and just an overall bad attitude." He shrugs.

All of which solidify my thoughts from last night. I don't believe Taylor has the backing that he's boasting he does. He's just an enraged child running around.

"Thanks, Jake. I'll have Ryder send over the new documents when they're ready, and I'll see you tonight at the fundraiser."

Jake tips his hat towards me with a chuckle as I walk back to the SUV and climb in. Thomas has the heat blasting, which is nice since I forgot to bring gloves. I hold my hands up to the vents as he turns us around to head back to the city.

My phone starts buzzing on the seat next to me. I glance at the screen before I answer it. "Ryder?"

"Well, did you get the contract?" he asks.

"Yes. It was never an issue, but he does want to expand some. I have more details that I'll type up in an email, so you can draft a new contract. He is going to need new designs once our designer starts."

I can hear him plop onto a leather couch. "Great news. Except, we don't have a designer yet. I hope you didn't give him a deadline anytime soon."

"I told him a couple weeks and we would have it."

"You did what!" A loud thud comes through the

phone. I grimace as he keeps yelling. "Fuck! Shit! What the hell? How are we going to find someone that's actually good, hire them, and get them to produce designs ready to see in a couple weeks? Are you insane? Motherfucker, I spilled coffee all over myself and the couch. You can't come at me with this kind of news when I'm not prepared." Ryder takes a breath. I can hear running water in the background.

"Stop being so stressed," I tell him. "I have everything under control. I just need you to make a new contract for Jake. I'll be back this afternoon. I need to stop at Collins and Sons before I come to the office." Thomas is chuckling to himself up front. No doubt he hears Ryder yelling through the phone.

"Yeah, right. Easy for you to say with all of your secrets. I'm going to have an aneurysm. I have to go home and change, I look ridiculous." Ryder huffs. "You should probably hire a cleaner for your office. Coffee is all over your couch. It's a mess. But it's also your fault."

I rub my temples. "Jesus, Ryder. Just ask Stacy to call one in. I'm kind of busy taking care of our other problems."

"Yeah, yeah. Fine. How was your night with Alex? I'm really bummed about poker night. Can we do it tonight instead?" he whines.

"If I get all of this figured out, then maybe." I regret the words as soon as they exit my mouth.

"Great! I'll set it up. Bye!" He clicks off the line before I can say anything else. I sigh and set my phone back on the seat. *He's going to be the death of me.* I pull up my email and go through the numerous updates from other clients during the rest of the drive.

I'm almost through my backlog of emails when Thomas clears his throat. "We have arrived at Collins and Sons."

I look out the window, and sure enough, we made it back. I rub a hand over my face. This is why I need a driver. It saves me so much time when I can continue to work while going places. I don't have to waste hours behind the wheel.

I grab my briefcase with my backup documents in the case Collins *is*, in fact, in on Taylor's scheme. I walk through the front door and lock eyes on the blonde receptionist. I quickly scan her desk in search of a name plate before I reach her. "Celest! I'm so sorry to interrupt your afternoon, but I need to speak with Mr. Collins."

She blinks up at me, clearly trying to figure out how I know her name, and if we know each other already. "Of course. Let me check his schedule ... What was your name again?"

I smirk. "James. James Edward."

Her face turns white with realization. I guess she has heard of me. Good. After a stunned moment, her head swivels back to her computer as she hazardously types and clicks around. "Umm. Just a minute. Let me see what he has planned."

"I could just go up there and check for myself. I'm

sure he wouldn't mind." I take a step to the side, and her hands shoots out at me.

"No no no. I'll just call up to him. One moment please." She picks up the phone and swivels her chair away from me. The moment he picks up, she whispers into the phone as fast as she can, peeking over her shoulder to ensure I haven't bolted for the elevator. I would never do that to her, but she doesn't need to know that.

I smile every time she looks back at me, which causes her to talk faster.

"Okay. I'll send him up." Celest gently sets the phone on the cradle and looks up at me. "Mr. Collins will see you now. His office is on the fifth floor, the corner suite."

I rap my knuckles on the desk. "Thank you, Celest. You've been amazing."

I make my way through security to the elevators as Taylor slams the main door open. It rattles against the wall but stays intact. I wave my fingers at him as I hit the button for the fifth floor.

"Where the fuck do you think you're going?" Taylor rushes across the lobby after me, but security stops him.

Celest stands up from her chair. "Taylor, you need to leave."

Taylor tries to push through the large muscle man they have for security, but he doesn't budge. "He can't go up there!... He..." The elevator doors click shut and gentle music starts playing as it travels me up towards the top floor.

A ding echoes right before the doors slide open and a short man with gray hair in his fifties steps towards me. "James, I wasn't expecting you," Collins says as he reaches out his hand.

I shake it firmly before looking down my nose at him. "Unexpected visits tend to happen when you start trying to poach my clients, especially the ones who have been with me from the start."

The confusion on his face makes me pause. "Let's go to my office and figure this out." He glances over his shoulder at the open offices surrounding the elevator, but doesn't say anything more.

I follow him down the hall to the corner suite where windows line every external wall and the view of the city is spectacular. The sun reflects off the river to the East with snow lining the shore. Collins motions for me to sit on the chair in the middle of his living room-like set-up, while he sits in the chair adjacent, leaving the couch open. He reaches towards the phone in the center of the table between the furniture and dials. It rings three times before a man picks up. "Yeah?"

"My office. *Now*." He hangs up and throws me a sympathetic smile, but I just sit back and wait to see what's going to happen next.

I turn towards the door when it snicks open. A mousey looking boy barely in his twenties steps through, and another slightly older version of him follows behind as they shuffle to the couch.

Collins looks at the boys with disdain. "What have you two idiots been up to?"

The older one elbows the younger in the ribs. "Ouch, Josh. Could you not?"

"This is your fault, Bobby." Now Bobby slaps Josh across the head.

"I didn't tell her to go fuck that idiot!" Bobby yells at his brother.

"Enough! I asked you a question." Collins throws a coaster at Bobby and nails him in the face. It's really hard to keep my composure.

"Ugh! What the f..." His dad shoots him a death glare. "Hell. I was going to say hell." Josh elbows him again. "Motherf—." He looks at his dad and stops. "It wasn't us."

"What do you mean? What wasn't you?" Mr. Collins is getting red in the face. I lean back in my chair and enjoy the show. Josh lifts his arm to hit Bobby again, but Collins jumps to his feet. "I asked you morons a fucking question!"

It's Josh's turn to look like he's going to get beat when I leave here. "We just made a bet. You wanted more clients, so your princess, Clair, decided we should see who could get the most first. It's not our fault she's cheating and using some other guy to do it."

"Clair?" Collins' face turns more white than red. "Where is she?"

"Uh. I don't know. Probably with that guy?" Bobby slides down the couch.

Yelling starts in the hall, and I crane my neck to get a better look of what's happening now.

"What in the actual fuck is going on in my business?" Collins points at the boys on the couch. "Stay, idiots." Collins opens the door to his office, and I spot Taylor speed walking down the hall with Celest and the giant trailing after him.

"Taylor, get back here! I've told you, you can't come up here without an appointment!" Celest yells.

"I'm going to make Mr. Collins millions. I think the least he can do is not listen to that dumbass James over me," Taylor shoots over his shoulder.

*Well, this is going to get interesting.* Collins holds a hand up. "It's fine. Celest and Bruno, you can go back down, so I don't have any more guests coming upstairs. I need a fucking minute to deal with this shit-show."

# CHAPTER 21
## *Alexandra*

I WAKE up to an empty bed. Again. "This is getting old."

I look around the room, but everything looks the same as it did when I passed out last night.

I look at my phone and see there are texts from Jaz and Ashlyn.

> Jaz: Are you alive?

> Ashlyn: Yeah. Hello? We would like to see these epic paintings.

> Ashlyn: And girls night.

> Ashlyn: And we have an event to go to.

> Jaz: Hello?

Jesus. I need to be better at checking my phone. I

scroll to James's thread, but there's nothing new there. I go back to the group chat.

> Alexandra: I'm alive. I'm at James's penthouse…

> Ashlyn: WHAT!

> Jaz: Details?

> Ashlyn: How did that happen! I need information!

I bite my lip. There's way too much to text. I leave the bedroom and check the rest of the apartment, but it's quiet.

> Alexandra: He's not here. Top floor of the Gatlyn, ask the doorman to let you up. I'm sure you can tell Ryder to add you to a list.

> Ashlyn: Talk no further. We will be there.

> Jaz: Stoked.

I go back to the bedroom and look through the small duffel bag I packed. I pull out fresh yoga pants and a sweater before going to his master bathroom with my toiletries. *Ugh.* My hair is sticking out all over and my mascara is running under my eyes.

*I really should have cleaned my face before going to bed.*

I do a rush job washing my face and brushing out my

wild tangles, so I look somewhat presentable and not freshly rolled in the sheets.

A banging at the front door has me running out of the room and sliding on the slick marble floors in my socks. "Shit." I barely catch myself on the kitchen counter when I round the corner. "Coming!" I yell as the banging ensues. This apartment is huge. I lightly jog the rest of the way, then flip the locks, so I can whip the door open.

"Oh, good. You look normal." Ashlyn is holding a breakfast pizza in one hand and a tray of coffees in the other. I tilt my head at her, but she just shrugs before handing me the drink tray and walking in. "What? I was hungry. Also, I need something to entertain my mouth while you tell me how the fuck all of this happened." She waves a hand at the massive apartment.

I hold the door open further, so Jaz can enter without running me over. "I honestly don't know what's happening right now." I groan into my hands.

"No offense, babe, but it kind of looks like you're with James now." Jaz also motions to the apartment we are all standing in.

"Maybe we should go to the couch. This is a much longer conversation," I say as I look over to Ashlyn who is half a slice in. Jaz grabs the box from her and follows me into the giant living room.

"Okay," Jaz drags out, looking at the screen taking up the wall. "What does James do again?"

"Umm. He's in marketing," I say. "He works for the

largest company in the industry, and him and his cousins are in charge of setting up this location in Shadowbrook."

Jaz narrows her eyes at me. "Right."

Ashlyn taps her hand on my leg. "Alright. Spill. What is happening?"

I curl my legs under my butt, getting comfortable. "It all started when I went to that cabin ..."

I quickly fill them in on the PG-13 details of my vacation and then everything with Taylor up to now. "So ... yeah. He wants me here to keep me safe."

Jaz just blinks at me. Ashlyn sits quietly which is very odd for her.

I twist my fingers around each other. "Say something."

I swear Jaz's brown eyes roll to the back of her head. "I could literally slap you sometimes, but that's Ash's job."

Ash chuckles as Jaz comes to sit in front of me, placing a hand on both of my cheeks, holding my attention. "That man does not want you here just to keep you safe. You know that, right?"

"But I just got out of a relationship. I know he says we are inevitable sometimes, but is this smart? Am I just being a relationship hopper again? Where is he?"

"Did you text him? You said there's drama with Taylor, so maybe he has to do something with that for his job?" Ash shrugs. "Why else would he leave you in this massive apartment? A sex suite, if you will."

"Oh my god." I hide my face in my hands. "You aren't helping."

"Well, you also forgot about that event your mom and my parents are making us go to tonight ... Didn't you?" Ash asks.

"Shit. What am I going to wear? And what about James?"

Ash's phone dings at the same time as mine. I pick it up, nervous energy coursing through me. I swipe it open and instantly deflate.

> Mom: There's an event tonight. You are expected to come. I've already told everyone you are attending. Don't disappoint me. Your sister told me you quit your job, so I know you don't have plans. It's a formal event. Look nice.

"James will be at the event," Ash says.

I peer over to her. "How do you know?"

She waves her phone at me. "Ryder just texted saying they are all busy tonight. I asked if he wanted to go to Club X earlier. He claims it's a business thing, so they're all going to be there. Especially since this is the elite's biggest auction and ball of the year."

I stare at her. Jaz continues to munch on her pizza.

"What?" Ash asks. "I follow all of the business dealings and events, even if I'm actively avoiding everything to do with my parents. As for the outfits, we brought everything. It's in the entryway. We figured you forgot since you didn't bother to mention it in the messages."

"You could just text James and ask him when he will be back, you know?" Jaz gives me a pointed look.

"Eh. That's too easy. We both know Alex here loves a challenge. Plus, looking really hot at an event sounds like a great way to figure out what else is going on here besides hot sex," Ash adds.

"Ash!" I throw a pillow at her, which bounces off her hand causing the pizza to splat onto the table.

She gapes at it in horror. "Rude." She picks it up, looks it over, and takes another bite. I scrunch my nose at her as she looks at me. "What? It wasn't dirty."

"I can't with you. But if we are going to go to the ball, then we'd better get ready. I'm going to need all the help I can get."

They each stuff another couple more pieces of pizza in their mouths, then we carry our coffees towards the bedroom. Ash hands me her cup and takes off to grab the dresses.

"What is this ball even for?" Jaz asks.

"Uh, let me ask mom what it's called. I think it's basically a huge auction for charity. That's why mom is a part of it, ever since Dad left she's been involved in his old-money charities. And she was able to keep her place when they got the divorce. I think it was part of the agreement. I really don't know. I try to stay out of it."

My phone buzzes, so I look down.

Mom: The Fireside Ball. It's a huge event with a lot of big names coming to present then mingle after. You better not back out, Alexandra. I told you I already told people you were coming.

"Something called the Fireside Ball." I look up and see Ashlyn is grinning at me like the Cheshire cat. "Fuck me."

She keeps grinning and nods. "Quite possibly, yes. That could be really hot though. You and James connecting in the coat closet of the event."

Heat creeps up my neck to my cheeks, and I look away. *Yeah, that would be hot, but I'm not sure it would actually happen.*

"Hello, hello?" Ryder's voice echoes through the main part of the apartment.

I whisper to Ash, "What the fuck?"

She just shrugs and walks back out of the bedroom. "What are you doing here?"

I follow behind her and see Ryder standing in the middle of the kitchen. "You texted, so I figured I would check on you." He hikes a thumb over his shoulder. "I live downstairs, so I just took the elevator. What are you guys up to?"

He tries to peek into the bedroom, but Jaz shuts the door when she comes out. "Uh, just working on getting ready."

His boyish smirk is contagious. "For what my dear?" He checks his watch, then says, "Isn't it a little early in the day to get ready?"

"The ball, you nosey man," Ash huffs, then flips her hair over her shoulder. "Beauty takes time, Ryder, and there's a lot to do. Along with catching up on the latest gossip."

"Oh! That's exciting. Does James know you're going?" he asks.

"I haven't seen him." I shrug. "I was told to go by my mother, so I figured if he goes too then I'll see him there."

He looks Ash up and down. "Interesting."

She looks down at her band T-shirt then back at him. "What?"

"Oh nothing. I just can't wait to see what you all look like when you get there." Ryder slides his hands into his pockets. Jaz sips her coffee while her eyes dart from Ryder to Ashlyn.

I clear my throat. "Do you happen to know why he isn't back yet?"

Ryder's head snaps over to me. His lips turn up in a grimace, his hand pulling on his neck. "Uh, he's still doing business stuff. I don't really know the details." Ash elbows him in the ribs and Ryder pretends to be severely wounded. "What! It's best if James tells her. It will come across a lot better. Plus, I enjoy my balls right where they are, thank you."

Ashlyn glares at him, but the second he starts batting

his lashes at her, she giggles and smacks his arm. "Quit that shit," she says.

"Why? Afraid you might fall in love with me?" Ryder asks. My eyes are flitting back and forth, waiting for them to make out already. Ryder slides the tips of his fingers up Ashlyn's arm. I watch her suck in a breath before she bats him away.

Her walls slam down and the sly attitude comes out. Arms crossed, smirk in place, and determination in her eyes. The armor I've watched her wear for years, ever since the night that destroyed her heart and her ideas of love and soulmates vanished. I deflate. *Nothing will be happening between these two anytime soon.*

She taps his nose. "Not a chance. Don't worry, it's inevitable for you to fall, they all do. I'll try to be gentle when *your* heart breaks."

I'm about to pull her away, but Ryder beats me to it. A flash of hurt crosses his eyes, but he too shoves walls into place, like it never happened. "Ah, my heart can't break, dear. I lost it a long time ago." He backs towards the door. "I'll see you beautiful ladies at the ball!" He blows us a kiss, closing the door softly on his way out.

Jaz claps her hands together. "We better get to work. We can't go to the ball dressed like this." She waves her hand at our pizza and coffee outfits that consist of cozy sweats. I frown, picking at my sweater. *Ugh, she's right.*

I look over at Ashlyn, whose smile is so big it's mirroring a kid on Christmas morning. She's in her element, and I'm going to be plucked and glitter bombed until I run away.

I walk towards her, accepting my fate.

She and Jaz start giggling, and I pretend to roll my eyes, even with a smile tugging at my lips.

"Let's go then."

# CHAPTER 22
## James

THE MEETING with Collins took a lot longer than I had hoped. It's technically still not finished. I threw an envelope of legal documents at him after hours of that shit show. Collins has a lot of house cleaning to do at his company, and I don't have the time or care to witness it all.

Alester checked all of our contracts and most have a clause that they can't just jump ship without cause and notice. He also found a bunch of legal problems within the Collins and Sons company, so he added those to the envelope for fun. By the time I got to the apartment building I needed to get changed and get to the ball. I was hoping I could convince Alex to come, but she wasn't there. Just a note on the counter that said, 'See you soon.'

I sent her a couple texts, but they've all gone unanswered.

The Fireside Ball is just a massive event where people

with money can flaunt around comparing dicks as they overbid on items for auction. The only reason I'm here and not chasing after Alex is because Ryder and Alester demanded it's good for the company to show ourselves and mingle with the clients that will be present. I also don't mind donating, since all proceeds go to the local fire department and helping orphaned children in the area.

Ryder is already following around the servers carrying snacks trying to take an entire tray. I shake my head at him and scan the room for Alester. He's seated at our table, waiting for the auction, as an elderly woman leans close, talking his ear off.

I laugh to myself as I continue scanning the room. A few clients are sprinkled around the room, big names that fill our books for years and allow us to take on smaller clients at a discounted rate, like Family Farms. I'll have to mingle with them after the auction.

The door to the auction room slams open, causing half the room to look towards the ruckus, and I turn to take in the scene as well. I chuckle to myself as I see Ashlyn stomping through the door in a silver dress with her heels so high I'm impressed she doesn't break her ankle. Jaz follows behind her in a navy dress, waving awkwardly at the people watching. I crane my neck waiting for the third in the trio, my Alexandra.

Her fingertips gently push the door open. I watch her black-studded heels step through as my eyes travel from her toes up her toned legs showing through the thigh high slit in her bright red dress. I hold my breath as I take in the mesh dip between her breasts going almost to her stomach. Her cleavage is on display demanding to be worshipped, but only by me.

I make my way across the room to her. Her long brown hair is styled in loose curls over one shoulder, and her eyes are latched on my body, eating me up with the same fire I have burning for her. *Fuck the ball. I want to take her out of here now.*

I stop just shy of pulling her body flush against mine, but barely.

Alex bats her long lashes at me. "God, how am I supposed to focus when you look like that?" She bites her lip, and I have to fight the urge to scoop her in my arms and haul her out of here like the caveman I am.

My voice is husky with need. "Me? Did you pass a mirror before you came here? It's taking all of my control not to throw you over my shoulder and leave this place."

That beautiful flush crawls up her light skin, and I can't help but brush my fingers against her arm, causing her to shiver and lean into my touch. Her eyes flutter closed as she almost whispers, "If that's true, then why did you leave without saying anything, again?" Her big brown eyes plead at me, and it makes my heart feel like it's breaking.

I cup her cheek. "Baby, that had nothing to do with you."

She leans into my touch and puts her hand on my chest. "Then what was it?"

I look down at her delicate hand. This woman would never do anything to hurt me, I feel it deep in my core. "I had meetings set up to ensure Taylor wasn't able to poach clients for Collins and Sons. Apparently the woman he cheated on you with is Collins's granddaughter. She isn't involved in the business, but she thought she would have a shot if she could get Taylor to take clients from my company. One of which was a client who my dad had the idea of partnering with." She watches me with an understanding I didn't believe another person could give me and that I'm not sure I deserve. "I couldn't let another part of him get pulled away from me, so I left without thinking at the cabin. Then this morning you just looked too adorable to wake." I press my forehead to hers. "I'm sorry, I should have woken you."

Alex threads her fingers behind my neck, pulling me closer to her and pressing her lips to mine. It's a gentle caress at first, but once I have a taste, I can't stop. I slip my tongue between her lips, her vanilla taste taking over all of my brain power, and then she moans. *Fuck. I'm not strong enough for this.*

Someone coughs, and I'm barely able to pull myself away from Alex's delicious mouth. Her eyes slowly open to me like she's caught in the same haze. "It's okay," she finally says.

She presses her entire body against me, and a growl rumbles up my throat. I look down at her. "If you keep pressing against me like this, I'm going to have to carry you out of here. Now."

That blush returns to her cheeks as she takes a micro-step backwards. "We can't have that. I promised my mom I'd make an appearance. Thank God you're here. Now I won't have to be set up with all the men I'm sure she has lined up."

My anger rushes to the surface, thinking of someone else touching what's mine. I pull her back against me. "Yeah, that's not going to happen."

She smiles up at me. "I thought you said I couldn't be this close?" She starts batting those damn eyes at me again.

I shrug. "I'll just walk around with my dick hard and everyone can have a nice show." She laughs and wiggles her hips against me. I take her chin in my hand, making her go still. I move my mouth a breath away from her lush lips. "Don't tempt me, Alex. I will lift that gorgeous dress and show everyone that I belong to you. I don't give a damn. Everyone *will* know you're mine."

I watch her pupils dilate. She presses her perfect breasts against my chest, letting me feel the quickening pace of her heart. A soft whimper slips past her lips, and I smile before taking her mouth against mine. She's perfection, and I can't imagine my life without her in it.

I'm about to drag her out of here and go home when a throat clears from behind her. Alex panics and pulls away from me, smoothing her hair back over her shoulder and wiping around her mouth like she's worried her makeup is messed up.

"You're beautiful, don't worry." I tip her chin up

with my fingers and place a soft kiss on her lips, so she relaxes.

The throat clears again. "Alexandra, seriously? I invited you to this ball so you could meet someone respectable. Not so you could make out with some man right before the auction." The woman scoffs. "Just a disappointment. Come now. We will go to the restroom and get you cleaned up."

The woman reaches for Alex's arm, but I slide in front of Alex effectively blocking the woman's hand unless she wanted to grab my abs. "Alex is right where she belongs, thank you," I say as I intertwine my fingers through Alex's hand. I glance down, and she looks like a deer in headlights with her eyes glued open darting back and forth from me to the woman. She obviously knows her, but at this point I don't care. No one needs to talk to Alex like that.

The woman huffs and raises her voice. "Excuse me, who do you think you are?"

Alex grimaces. "Mom. Stop."

I look between them now, trying to see the resemblance, but I can't see anything that screams Alex in this woman. It's obvious from her tone and Alex's posture folding in on herself that they don't have a great relationship, and that's all I need to know.

I put my hand out for her to shake, always the businessman. "I'm James, Alex's boyfriend." Alex gawks at me, but I feign ignorance. "What'd I say? Would you rather, lover? Hot side piece? Boo thing forever? Or are we jumping right to it and calling me your husband? Because, let's be honest, that's where ..."

Alex throws her hand over my mouth, and I have to resist the urge to lick it.

"Jesus, James. We can talk about your crazy labels later."

I nod. She waits a minute, not trusting me to keep my mouth shut. *Fair.* Then she removes her hand, turning to her mother. "Mom, this is James. James, this is my mom."

Her mom lifts her nose in the air. "You may call me Mrs. Lewis. I wasn't aware you had a new boyfriend, Alexandra."

"It just sort of happened." Alex responds. Everything about Alex is now short and to the point. Not the brave, artistic woman I got to know at the cabin.

Before her mom can chew her ass for whatever she believes is her job within Alex's love life, I interject. "I'm terribly sorry, but I have a lot of business I need to tend to tonight, and I'd like Alex to meet everyone."

I give Mrs. Lewis the small smile I use in difficult business meetings and lace Alex's hand through my arm, walking away.

# CHAPTER 23

## Alexandra

MY MIND IS SPINNING in a whirlwind. I can't even function with my mom and James in the same room. I mean I knew they would both be here, but mentally I wasn't ready. James seems to feel it, or he just wants me closer because he wraps his arm around me, pulling me tight to his side. There are so many people around I'm starting to panic a little.

James veers us to the right, opens a door to the fanciest bathroom I've ever seen, and ushers me inside. I hear a lock click behind me then his arms are circling me again, and he spins me to face him. "Hey, are you okay?"

I press my hands to his chest and try to match my heartbeat to his. "I will be." I slide my hands to the back of his neck and pull his mouth down to mine. He kisses me, slow and soft, before pulling back.

"Alex?" James looks into my eyes, searching.

"James." I trail my hands down his chest to his suit jacket and start undoing the buttons.

His breathing increases. "What are you doing, babe?"

I stop and look up at him through my lashes. "Well, I'm going to calm myself down by using my new *boyfriend*." I watch his eyes dilate as he takes in what I'm saying. I almost laugh, but I'm able to hold it in. "Unless …"

His voice is husky with need. "Unless what?"

"Unless you don't want it?" I take a step back, but his hands snap out latching onto my hips and pulling me flush against his chest.

"There is no world where I wouldn't want you, Alex." My heart skips. I stop breathing, lips parting. I don't know what to say. But it doesn't matter because his mouth is on mine in an instant. His hands slide down my hips, cupping my ass as he lifts me, and backs me up until I feel a cold counter slide underneath me. I reach blindly, fumbling as I unclasp his belt and slack buttons before freeing him.

Banging on the door behind James has me laughing. James covers my mouth with one hand while he expertly slides my dress up with the other. "Sorry babe, we are going to have to be quick before they go get the master key." Before he can finish his sentence, he's slamming into me causing my laugh to turn into a moan. He keeps his hand secured across my mouth, muffling my sounds, as he hits that delectable spot with each thrust. I come with a scream, my pent-up energy releasing from my body like a shock wave. His movements escalate, causing my orgasm to continue to rock my body as he comes inside of me, shaking from the sheer force.

A muffled curse comes from behind the door as the person hits it one more time and stomps away, finally giving up. I let a halfhearted giggle loose as I rest my head against James's shoulder trying to catch my breath.

He holds me, rubbing small circles across my back. "Are you feeling better, love?" When he feels me nod against his shoulder, he slowly slides out of me with a hiss and goes to the sink. A moment later, he comes back with a warm wet cloth and kneels between my legs.

"What are you doing?"

I feel the cloth press against my sensitive flesh. "Cleaning you, remember? I made you dirty, so now I'm going to make sure you're nice and clean." His fingers replace the cloth as he slides into me, curling the tips making my head fall back.

"And ... this?" I ask, barely able to breathe.

His strokes continue. "I need to get my semen out of you, so you're not uncomfortable the rest of the night. Just relax."

And I do. I let him pull every drop of himself out of me while I climb another crest. The second orgasm slams through me. My knees are shaking, but he doesn't stop until I'm writhing under his touch. He slowly slides his fingers from me, then reaches for a fresh cloth. I jolt as the fabric touches my sensitive skin.

"Easy, Baby. I've got you," he says.

I slide off the counter letting my dress fall to just above my heels. The silky material glides across me like a light touch, leaving me shivering. Spinning, I check my makeup in the mirror and pull my nude lip liner out of my clutch to put on another light layer. I smooth my hair and smirk at James as he stands just behind me, watching. "You're spectacular." He presses a kiss to the back of my head. "Are you ready to brave the crowd again?"

He holds his hand out to me, so I place mine on top. He spins me towards him, chest to chest. "Let's do it."

I push my shoulders back, spine straight, and let him lead us out of the restroom. *I can't believe we just did that, but damn am I glad it was with James. I don't think I could ever feel as safe as I do when I'm with him.*

His smile is blinding when he looks at me, and I feel like I can walk on top of the world.

No one looks towards us when we leave, which frankly, shocks the hell out of me. I expect it to be more like the movies where everything stops, music to a halt, and they turn knowing exactly what happened in that bathroom. But everyone continues with their conversations and meals as James leads us to the far table in the front row. I notice his cousins are already seated with Jaz and Ashlyn at the table. Ashlyn flashes me a smile before diving back into her conversation with Ryder. Alester is sitting on the other side of Ryder looking into a glass of whiskey while Jaz is flailing her arms wildly talking to an older woman sitting next to Alester. I know what those arms mean—research. Luckily the woman looks like she's enraptured with Jaz's project, which I'm sure she's going into great detail about. The girl loves her science.

"Wow. Great of you to finally show up, cousin!" Ryder jumps up to hug James with one arm.

James grunts, returning the gesture. "I've been here. Just around. You know, mingling."

Ryder cocks his head and looks James up and down. "Riigghhtt." He drags it out dramatically, and I feel heat blazing my cheeks.

Ryder looks at my reddening face but quickly glances back to James with a straight face. "I'm sure I must have missed you. I lined up a couple of meetings with potential clients for next week. A lot of people are interested in the new meat in town. Well, the ones that didn't already know of the company from the New York branch."

James laughs, shaking his head. "You're gross, but that's great news. Maybe we can drop the other one if our numbers align."

Ryder purses his lips but shrugs.

Ashlyn reaches over, pulling me down to the chair next to her. "Sit, I have to know everything."

"What do you mean by *everything*?" I laugh.

She sits back dramatically, clutching her chest. "Alexandra! You dirty girl. Obviously, *everything*, everything. But you can start with the PG things for now."

We both double over laughing. Ryder drops back down in his vacated chair as James pulls the one next to me a tad closer, putting his arm across the back of my chair. "What's so funny?" Ryder asks, leaning right in front of Ashlyn's face.

She pushes his forehead back. "Mind your business."

Ryder pretends to be wounded while James and I chuckle at them. "Excuse me, but this is my table that I invited you to. So therefore, everything at this table is my business," he says as a matter of fact.

James leans forward to look at Ryder,."Actually, this is my table."

"Stay out of it." Ryder playfully snaps back.

The tapping of a mic pulls everyone's attention to the front of the room. "If you'll excuse me, we are ready to start the auction. We are going to start tonight off with one year of free advertisement generously gifted from The Edward Corporation."

There's quiet murmuring all around. I look around the room trying to figure out where the owner of the company is seated as they have to be present for the auction, but various tables are pointing at us.

I lean over and whisper at James, "Why is everyone pointing at this table?"

His answering smirk is interrupted by the announcer. "We will start the bid at five million dollars." He points to a man holding a paddle. "Five million, do we have six?" Another paddle goes up and another.

My mind is reeling. What in the hell? I feel James's breath on my ear before I hear him. "They're pointing because the owners of The Edward Corporation are at this table." I turn to look at him with wide eyes, my mouth falls open. "I'm James *Edward*."

"What the fuck do you mean?"

I turn so we are face to face. I watch as his smile gets bigger. "I mean what I said. It's my company. I have the largest share then Ryder and Alester split the rest."

I blink at him a few times, trying to comprehend just how much money these three are worth. "Wait. I thought you just worked for them? Why wouldn't you correct me?"

"People sometimes act differently when they know I have the kind of money I have. So, I usually avoid bringing it up." He places a hand on my thigh with the slit. His thumb rubbing circles on my bare skin. "It wasn't a secret. Just a precaution I tend to take with everyone ever since Rebecca."

"Hmm."

He leans closer to me. "What are you thinking?"

"I really don't fucking understand why you don't have a full-size generator for the cabin now."

His head drops back in a deep belly laugh, and soon I'm joining in.

I feel my overly full stomach after the five-course meal they served alongside the auction. "I think this dress is at its capacity."

James looks at me, mortified. "It's a brownie!"

"And I think I'm going to pop all of my seams if I eat that brownie."

He blinks at me slowly before sliding off his jacket, then motions for me to put my arms in the sleeves sliding it over my back and buttons it. He picks up the brownie and holds it in front of my mouth. "Now you can eat it, and if the seams do break, you're covered."

He waits, watching my mouth, so I open with a giggle and let him feed me. *Mmmm, he's right. This is the softest brownie I've ever had.* I close my eyes, savoring the rich chocolate melting in my mouth, the sweetness coating my tongue. I feel like I'm floating in a sea of sugar. I love it.

"I'm getting you another one. That was the hottest thing I've ever seen." My shoulders shake with laughter as he jogs towards a server circling the room with a tray hovering over her shoulder. He swings around her blocking her path, and swipes five more brownies before jogging back to me. We are in the large ballroom. People are still filtering in from the auction room, ready to start business discussions and strike deals outside of the office. "Alright. Part those lips for me again, babe."

I'm glad my friends are engrossed in other conversations because I'm sure I'd never hear the end of the comments if they could hear James talking to me now. I do as I'm told and open my mouth, never breaking eye contact as James slowly slides the brownie past my lips. I bite down on the gooey chocolate and moan as it melts in my mouth again.

"Dammit, Alex. We need to get out of here."

# CHAPTER 24
## James

I THINK brownies are my new favorite treat. I coax Alex into eating one more before she's shooing me away. All I had to do was show them to Ryder and he ate them all before I could blink.

Alex is chatting with Jaz and Ashlyn when her mom starts walking towards me. I meet her halfway. "Mrs. Lewis."

"James, or should I say owner of The Edward Corporation?" I don't acknowledge the jab, so she continues huffing her chest. "I can't believe you didn't bother to mention that little tidbit earlier. Or that my daughter didn't either in that case. I'm truly surprised she would consider a relationship with you."

She's clearly wanting some sort of reaction from me. "Why's that?"

She scoffs. "Lord knows I've been trying to set that girl up with." She looks me up and down, "someone of your standing for years, but she's always denied me. Tonight, I had a few introductions planned for her, but then she shows up with you. It's very peculiar."

"I can assure you, ma'am, that Alex just learned about my business tonight."

"Yeah, right. That girl." Shaking her head, she looks over to Alex laughing with her friends. "I love her and want the best for her. But she's always had a dreamer's mind. She can't be happy just pushing papers around and making a nice income, no. Not my Alex. She wants to be risky and wild forever." She looks back to me, sadness creeping across her face. "Maybe you can finally tame her."

I take in my girl in her red dress, black heels, her hair is getting wilder by the minute, and she can't stop smiling and laughing with her friends. She's lighting up the entire world without even realizing it.

"No. I don't think I will."

Mrs. Lewis starts to open her mouth again, but I interject. "Magic like that deserves to be out in the world wild. It would be devastating to try and tame the flame that demands to burn uncontrolled. I will gladly burn with her and be a better man for it." Her mouth hangs open like a goldfish. "If you'll excuse me, I see a business partner I need to talk to." Jake from Family Farms just walked up to our little group of misfits.

"—just show the man your current painting. He obviously wants to see what you can do," Ashlyn says lightly, shoving Alex.

I watch that blush caress her neck as she pulls her phone out of her purse, sliding it open and handing the device to Jake. "It was recently rendered, and I'm still working on the digital file, but that's how it looks—"

"You painted this?" Jake looks up from the phone with wet eyes. Jake's been through a lot, kind of like me, so it's no surprise that Alex's talent brought emotion out in him.

I stand near Alex, but I make sure I don't over-shadow her moment. I remember seeing her pour her heart and soul into that painting, and she deserves this moment. Seeing others in awe of her talent.

"I—uh yes. I did."

"James," Jake scolds me.

"Jake."

"You didn't mention you already found a new designer during our last discussion." He looks to me then circles to Ryder and Alester who say nothing. Both of them shrug at me with a grin.

*Okay assholes.*

I sent them the half-assed photo I took of the canvas, but we've been too busy in crisis mode to really talk about anything. Seems like they've been talking plenty.

"Well, I haven't had time to present her with a job offer...yet."

Alex's head whips to me. "You what!"

Jake looks between us. "Seems like you have some explaining to do. We can talk more at our meeting next week. But James, make no mistake, I want her on my accounts. I need that emotional depth within my designs. I won't take no for an answer."

With that he walks away.

Alex's eyes bounce between the three of us. Ashlyn and Jaz are sipping from their drinks seemingly entertained. "What is happening?"

I pull Alex close to me, sick of the damn distance. *Finally.* "Alex, my lovely, lovely girlfriend. Will you please come work with myself, Ryder, and Alester at The Edward Corporation and be our full-time designer? You will have an office with a view, your choice of medium, and whatever other gadgets you may need." She stares, stunned, so I push my bottom lip out in a pout. "Pretty please?"

"You're serious?" She looks to my cousins, who both nod in return. Then she comes back to me.

"Dead serious. We don't joke about business." Again, she says nothing.

"For fuck's sake, Alex! Say yes! This is your fucking dream being laid out in front of you," Jaz spouts. She looks like she might throw her drink at Alex if she tries to say no.

"Yeah, bitch. You know you want it. It's all you've talked about since moving here. This is your chance to shine. Or paint or whatever." Ashlyn says.

Alex takes in everyone around us, contemplating, maybe panicking.

"Come on, let's take a walk." I pull her with me across the floor. When it's just us, she relaxes in my arms.

"You can say no if you want to. I wanted to gift you an impressive offer that you could take your time with and go through, but well, plans never really go how we expect them to." I shrug, pulling us to a stop near a pillar away from prying eyes.

She lets go of the breath she was holding. "Two questions."

"Shoot."

"Is there a rule against inter-office dating?"

I throw my head back laughing and pull her tightly against my body, where we fit perfectly. "No, babe. And if there were, I'd shred it. Next."

She smirks up at me, "How good *is* the benefits package? Because if I could get a bigger apartment that would be cool."

I growl, "Alex..."

"James..."

I roll my eyes at her jokey tone. "I already told you. You're moving in with me. You scared me back there. I thought you were going to bolt or tell me to go fuck myself." I run my hands up and down her arms. "You'll really take it? Because your talent is unmatched, and I can't think of another person who would fit this role and the company better than you and your wild self."

"Is there a dress code?" She wiggles in my arms when I attack her with tickles. "Okay, okay! I yield! Sorry!" I halt my attacking fingers, pressing her against me, so she has to crane her neck back to look me in the eyes. "Yes, I will help you and your family by making you the best damn designs you've ever seen."

"Thank God. You're going to get spanked for drawing out the suspense." I wink at her as we start wandering back towards our group.

"Maybe I'll like it." She winks.

*What am I going to do with this woman?*

"Well?" Ryder asks when we're back.

"Yes, yes. I will be your lovely designer. I expect great parking and coffee."

Ryder laughs, pulling her from me to hug her. Alester's lips pull up, just barely. "Anything for you. I'm sure we can rearrange some spots." His eyes shoot daggers at me over Alex's head.

"Dammit." I have a feeling I just lost my fancy parking spot. Not that it matters since Thomas drives me, but on the off chance I do drive myself, I had a spot. I pull Alex in close and kiss the top of her head then lean down to whisper in her ear, "Did you like your surprise?"

She turns in my arms, her eyes lined with confusion. "What surprise?"

It dawns on me then that I rushed out the door for the meetings and forgot to leave a note. "Shit." I pull on the back of my neck.

"What is it?" she presses.

"It's at the apartment. It will be better if you see it."

The ball is in full swing, people mingling and dancing around.

Alex pouts. "You can't just tell me?"

"I—" I pause as a blonde woman comes rushing over.

"Alex! I can't believe you're actually here! I mean, when mom told me, I thought she was imagining it." Alex steps towards the blonde as she smashes into her. They both teeter in their high heels but catch each other.

"Annabel, what are you doing here? Don't you have classes?" Alex laughs as they pull apart.

"You know Mom. Classes can wait when there's possible suitors. Speaking of suitors..." She peeks around Alex towards me. "Who is that?" she whispers.

Alex laughs then grabs my hand. "This is James. James, this is my sister, Annabel."

"It's nice to meet you," I say as she rakes her eyes over me.

"Possibly nice to meet you too. Was this a mom set-up?" Annabel asks, suspiciously.

Alex giggles, but I respond, "No. Actually, we've been bumping into each other for the last week, until she finally decided I might be worth it."

"He just met Mom tonight, and I don't think she was very happy with the idea that she wasn't the one to set me up again."

"Sounds like her." Annabel checks over her shoulder and groans. "Looks like she's looking for me. I better get back, but you better call me and tell me all of the details soon!"

"I will," Alex says as her sister scurries across the dance floor to their mother, who's staring over at us like she's about to tap her foot in annoyance. "Yikes. Can I go see that surprise now, or do you have more business things to do?"

"We can go." I walk over to Ryder and tap him on the shoulder. He spins from his conversation with Ashlyn. "We are heading out. Let me know if there are any other meetings you manage to secure for tonight, but we should be fine for now if you want to just enjoy the evening." I nod towards Ashlyn, but he subtly declines.

"Sounds good. I'll probably wait for Alester then we can all head out," Ryder says. I wish he would get out of his own head and take a chance on something long term. A relationship that's more than a night in the sheets.

I stand off to the side and wait as Alex tells her friends bye. The twinkle in her eyes as she saunters over to me makes me want to throw her over my shoulder, but that would give the whole room a show. I'd rather keep Alex all to myself. "Are you ready, my love?"

Her smile grows, dimples forming in her cheeks as she loops her arm through mine. "Completely."

We walk together across the room towards the front door and I wave at a few clients on our way. Thomas is chatting with some friends near the door when he spots us walking towards him. "Ready to go?" he asks.

"You can stay if you want, Thomas. We can take a cab," I offer.

"Nonsense. These fellows know the job. Plus, then I can get home early to my girls." He beams at me. "I'll go get the vehicle while you two get your coats from the coat check." Thomas makes his way through the ballroom doors and out front.

"Shall we?" I ask Alex.

"Sounds great." We walk together to the coat check. I give the man in charge of them our names then fold my arms around Alex. "Eventually you're going to get sick of constantly holding me."

I squeeze her tighter. "There's zero chance that could ever happen."

"I guess we will see."

The attendant comes back with our coats. I take Alex's white wool trench coat and slip it over her arms. Then I slowly button her up and tie the sash. I kiss the tip of her nose before I slide my black coat over my tux.

"Are you going to tell me what this surprise is?"

I take her hand as we walk out to the waiting SUV. "Not a chance. It's not that far away." I help her into the backseat before I make my way around to the opposite side. Thomas slides into the driver's seat. "You're going to love it ... Hopefully."

Alex giggles, threading her fingers with mine. "I'm sure whatever it is will be amazing." She rests her head on my shoulder for the twenty-minute drive to the apartment.

I'm itching with nervous energy. I hope I didn't hype this up too much in my head. It's too late now. I already told her about it, and Thomas is pulling up to the door. Surprises are a lot more nerve racking when you care so much about the person you're doing it for.

We ride in silence up to the top floor, and through the front door. She looks around the main living space. "Well, where is this top-secret surprise?"

I smirk at her smart-ass response and show her to the spare room on the east side of the apartment. I tap on the door and slide out of the way so she can open it.

"James. Nothing better jump out at me or I'll scream." She turns the door handle slowly, but I still stay silent. Alex swings the door inward and gasps. I follow her into the room and watch as she traces her fingers over the rose petals lining her new desk. Four bouquets of long stem roses are set up throughout the room. Three easels propped in various locations. She walks over to the shelving organizer against the wall that tried to best me this morning. She lifts various tubes of new paint and brushes of every size.

"Why?" Alex whispers as she glances over her shoulder, her eyes wet with unshed tears.

"Because I want you here, with me. I want every messy piece of you. I want you to chase your dreams without a worry of what's going to happen next. I can't wait to see every work in progress as you spend hours in front of a new canvas ... because I'm in love with you."

Tears spill down her cheeks, and she rushes into my open arms. "I love you, too."

# CHAPTER 25
## *Alexandra*

I KNOW I made a lot of jokes at the ball, but actually, bringing my art supplies to The Edward Corporation building is blowing my mind. I got here bright and early, the only other person at the office is Stacy, and I can already tell I'm going to love everything about her.

She met me in the lobby when security called up to her and escorted me personally to my office with a bright smile glued to her face. I've been unboxing my things since.

This office is huge. It's a corner suite with floor-to-ceiling windows on two of the full walls. My door is glass with a blurring feature. Stacy said it's for when I'm working on private client material. Apparently, the boys bring clients to the building for regular meetings and with this new location, they have clients that are closer like Family Farms, and continue to build their new client list within this location. Ryder is surprisingly good at his job from what Stacy told me.

A light knock on the door has me spinning towards the sound, almost dropping my lavender plant.

James stops right at my threshold. "You snuck out of bed."

I lean against my clean white desk. "It's my first day at a new job. I couldn't be late."

"I think your boss would understand." He crosses the room to stand in front of me.

I place my hands on his chest. "I don't want him to think less of me. I'm a hard worker. Plus, I'm excited to start working on *my* clients' new designs."

"*Your* clients, huh?" His cedar scent is intoxicating and I almost forget what we are talking about.

"Wha—Oh yeah. Stacy logged me into my new work email, and Jake already sent me some ideas he wants me to work on." I flip my screen around on the desk to show him.

James barely glances at the message before hovering above my lips. "I'm happy you're excited, Babe. Next time, wake me up so I can come with you."

"Deal." His lips brush mine, and I pull on his sweater to get him closer.

He backs out of my hold easily. "Nope. You have unpacking to do." I look at my mess of boxes and push my lip out in a pout. He laughs at me. "I have a coffee run to go to. My new employee negotiated good coffee as a work requirement." He shrugs and walks backwards out my office door while I squeal in delight.

*Damn, this is going to be a great job.*

I'm waiting outside Brick Stone Pizza when I see Ashlyn making her way down the sidewalk. "You made it! Where's Jaz?"

She hustles over to me in her stiletto heels. "Dunno. She just said she would get a ride from someone in her class."

A sports car screeches to a halt in front of the entrance. A tall man in glasses with a grey button-up shirt steps out, walks around the front of the car, and opens the passenger door while we stand stunned. A black jean leg pops out, followed by the rest of our best friend.

"What the—" Ashlyn gapes.

"Thanks for the ride, I'll see you later." Jaz waves at the man.

"Anytime, Jaz. You know I don't mind." He jogs

around to the driver's side, waving again to our Jaz before jumping in and peeling off like he's in a race.

"Hey, guys!" Jaz says as she walks up to us. "You didn't have to wait outside."

"Uh … What was that?" I ask, still trying to figure out what happened.

"*Who* is that!" Ash yells at the same time.

"What? Him? That's just Lenny. He's working in the same research building as me." She cocks her head to the side, eyeing us.

"Does Lenny drive you around often? I thought I was your taxi bitch?" Ash pretends to be offended.

Jaz throws her black hair over one shoulder, and rubs at her neck. "Yeah, sometimes. I usually have a lot of research to do at various locations, so he drives me to collect samples and do studies most days."

"Most days!" Ash's mouth almost hits the floor. "How am I just hearing about this? I thought we were close?"

"What?" Jaz asks.

"Are you guys dating?" I ask what Ash really wants to know.

Jaz doubles over laughing, she can barely breathe. "Excuse—me? Lenny? Jesus, no. We are just doing research in the same area. Not the same actual study, but our samples are located near each other, so we are saving gas by carpooling." She pulls the front door to the pizza place open. "You two are wild. Me and Lenny? Get real."

I look at Ash, and she shrugs at me. *Cool, we're both oblivious.*

We follow behind her into the building and back to our regular booth. We've been coming here weekly since we first became friends. The owner, Dom, gives us a free appetizer every time we show up because we remind him of his daughter who moved to Europe a few summers ago. He's been our adoptive dad ever since those first few weeks when he started stopping by our table to get the latest girl drama. He says girls have the best views on life, and he misses the daily entertainment from his daughter, so he likes stealing a bit from us when we're around.

Dom peaks over the back kitchen window at our table before waving. We wave back and slide into our spots.

"So, tell us, how's the office?" Ash asks after she slides in next to Jaz.

"Amazing. Honestly, this all feels like a fever dream. Am I dreaming? No, don't tell me." We decided to meet for lunch on my first day. I've already gone through a bunch of client debriefs and prepped content to make this week and it's only noon.

"You're a nut job. But I hope you're loving it. You deserve this. All of it." Jaz says.

"Yeah, we know your mom gets a little wild about the art scene, but we've seen your work for years. We know how talented you are, you just needed the right person to finally see it." Ash looks at me with her wildness creeping in again. "I guess it's a good thing, everything that happened when you quit. You know, finding Taylor at your apartment and everything. Maybe we should send him a card."

"Ugh. Why do you have to remind me!" I ball up a napkin and toss it at her, but she dodges it.

"Hey! I'm just saying, maybe it wasn't so bad. You know, carpe diem and all that jazz."

"What?" Jaz whips her head up from the menu.

"Not you, you dummy." Ash rolls her eyes. "No one listens to me."

I laugh and pat her hand. "It's okay. I know what you mean. Everything happens for a reason. Even if it sucks in the moment."

Dom rushes over and places water glasses in front of each of us, sliding an overflowing basket of breadsticks in the middle with a cup of cheese.

"Yesss! We love you, Dom!" Ash yells, while Jaz and I beam, diving for the bread.

"Best day *ever*," I say as I inhale my breadstick with cheese.

"Better than the cabin?" Ash asks around her bread.

I give her a death glare. "Okay, whatever, second best."

We all bust out laughing and try not to choke.

# Epilogue

## ALEXANDRA – ONE MONTH LATER

"ARE you going to tell me where we're going yet?" We've been driving for hours to this top-secret location, and James hasn't let a hint drop once.

He glances at me before his eyes go back to the winding road. "Patience. We are almost there, then you will have all of your questions answered."

The snow is almost completely melted from that wild storm. Now just a dusting is left across the grass. A couple of miles later we turn down a long driveway, each side surrounded by trimmed trees. It looks like something out of a movie, my head is swiveling around, trying to take it all in. At the end, it opens up to acres of yard with buildings strategically placed. A white barn sits off to the right, connected by fencing where cows graze. A large chicken coop is off to the left of the barn. Another large outbuilding sits directly off the driveway.

The house is tucked off to the left, and my breath

hitches. It's beautiful. A modern take on a wooden cabin, complete with a wraparound porch. The dark stain of the wood pairs nicely with the dark doors and windows. It looks a lot bigger than anything I've ever lived in. The porch furniture is a cozy green, the swing full of pillows. Flowers on the end table are freshly placed, as if someone is expecting us. There's no way anyone just leaves that out with this weather, even if it is relatively warm today.

I turn to him as he pulls around to park in front of the garage. "What is this place?"

He lets out a sigh, looking at the house. "This is my house. I haven't moved in yet, but I... I built it for my dad to finish out his days, initially. Unfortunately, he was only able to enjoy it for about a year." He opens the door and motions for us to get out. I step out, button my jacket, and put my gloves back on.

Our shoes crunch in the leftover snow as we walk across the yard, making our way towards the chickens. "When did he pass?" I ask.

"It's been about eight years now." He looks at the animals then out across the yard, a sadness radiating off him that I haven't seen. "He was my best friend, my biggest supporter, and the best damn father I could've asked for. My mom passed away when I was young, so it was always me and him. Well, my aunts, Ryder and Alester's moms, always tried to be around as much as they could, but it's not the same."

"I'd love to hear about him sometime, whenever you're ready. And your mom."

He looks back at me with a sad smile before I wrap my arms around his middle.

He kisses the top of my head. "Sometimes I come here to talk to him like he's still lingering. Like he can still hear me and give me advice. The sound of his voice floats on the wind, and if I listen hard enough, I can hear him. Or at least it feels like I can."

James reaches for my hand as he walks us back up to the front porch. I follow in silence, letting him decide what he wants to tell me.

The steps to the porch are clear of snow, a built-in fireplace set up in the corner is already full of wood and flames. The heat rolling off towards us makes it comfortable to stay on the porch and enjoy the outdoors even in the cold weather.

"This estate is set up the way he loved it. Animals to look at, a large yard, a big porch, plenty of space for future grandchildren." James leans against the railing, and I feel my heart breaking for him. "We came up with the idea for our company when he was in the hospital ... dying." He fiddles with the buttons on his coat, remembering.

I take in the beautiful property sprawled out behind him, imagining what could have been.

"Watching the cancer slowly kill him was bad, but when he asked me to let him go ..." His eyes fill with unshed tears. I don't have any words, so I go to him and wrap my arms around him as tight as I can. "He didn't want to fight anymore. His body and soul had had enough, and I couldn't be selfish and ask him to stay any longer. I sat with him, while they filled him with pain meds and his body slowly shut down at the end.

"When he was awake, we worked on the company, and when he slept, I kept working. Then one day he just stopped waking up. I stayed until they disconnected all the monitors and wheeled him away. I kept working, and I haven't stopped. My cousins hate that I live at the office, or that when I do venture to my apartment I never stop working, but I built this with my dad. I feel like if I stop working so hard then his memory will start to fade."

He turns towards me, brushing my hair behind my ear. "I know he wouldn't want me to work as much as I do, but it was the only thing helping my grief. Even with all of the time that has passed, all I can hear is him telling me the only way I'll be able to live my life is by going out and actually living." He shrugs. "He saw and did so much in his lifetime, but the few years before he passed I spent a lot of time just being with him and helping as much as I could while also in school. When we came up with the idea for The Edward Corporation, I dropped out and went full force into making it a reality. I feel like watching someone's future disappear makes you want to chase your dreams that much faster and harder. We never know when our last days will be."

I squeeze him tighter. "He would be so proud of everything you've built." I look back at the barn, the cows grazing. "This place is really magical. I can see why you say you feel him here. If this was a place built for me out of love, I don't think I'd be able to leave it either. I bet he watches the sun rise with the chickens and cows."

"Then at dusk he rocks in the chair, watching the sun set from the porch," he joins in, rocking us slightly as we stand by the railing.

I reach up, running my fingers through his hair, and pulling him down for a kiss I feel my soul seep into. He has all of me, mind, body, and soul, and he just gave me a piece of him that I will cherish forever.

"Thank you for bringing me here and telling me about your dad."

James kisses me again before taking me over to the porch swing. I curl into his side as we watch the sun set, him gently rocking us.

The sound of a vehicle coming down the driveway pulls us out of our moment. I peer over my shoulder at the approaching black SUV. "What's happening now?" I ask James as a smirk spreads across his face.

"I figured we might as well get used to the chaos now, since this will be our main home."

My eyes bulge. "Our what?"

James chuckles. "Well, I want you to redecorate or remodel as much as you want to make it yours too. But I don't want to live here without you."

I'm speechless, trying to wrap my head around this place, when car doors slam.

Ashlyn's voice echoes in the quiet. "This places is massive! I brought wine!"

"I picked up your favorite large chocolate chip cookies," Jaz adds.

Ryder jingles the metal case he's carrying. "I'm finally going to beat all of you at poker."

"Yeah, right." Ash nudges him with her shoulder, and he smirks down at her.

Alester comes up the steps behind them carrying four large bags. "We picked up Chinese food on the way, too."

All four of them go into the house, their voices echo through the walls, and I can't help but laugh. "Full chaos?"

James wraps his arms around me as he pulls me towards the door. "Why not? It's the only way with our people involved."

The dining room table sits near large windows, and it's already been converted to a full poker table layout. Ryder slid his baseball hat backwards as he sets up the decks and chips. Ashlyn is filling cups, while Alester and Jaz dish up plates of food for everyone.

This is going to get wild.

Thank you for taking a chance on my winter romance. I hope you enjoyed the world of Alexandra and James. Don't worry, Ashlyn and Jaz will be getting their own novels in the future! I can't wait to bring you more stories. There are a lot planned, so be sure to sign up for my newsletter to keep updated on everything coming next!

I couldn't have done this without my Beta team to sound off on and help me navigate through the various drafts. I think I would have gone insane.

I love my Street Team! They keep me motivated as they share and scream about my other books while I'm deep in editing mode! I love all of our random chats in the discord too. Thank you for choosing to be a part of this wild ride!

The most important people in all of this, my husband and son that have seen a lot of my computer lately! I appreciate and love both of you beyond belief!

I will be writing endless love stories for all of you readers that are willing to devour them. I'm so excited that you are choosing my words to read in your free time. I love you all!

K.P. Knupp received her Master of Science in Biology, specializing in microbiology, ecology, aquatic, and marine from the University of Houston–Clear Lake, she's currently living in Minnesota. In between work and spending time with her husband, son, and her wild German Shepherd, Nyx, she enjoys reading and writing. If there's time to spare, she enjoys creating stickers and mugs!

Contact K.P. Knupp

Instagram/Threads/TikTok: @KPKnupp

Website: kpknupp.com

Goodreads.com/kpknupp

Sign up for my Newsletter at https://kpknupp.com/mailing-list

## Snowed In at the Cabin

After Alexandra comes home from another failed interview, she catches her boyfriend of three months with another woman on her couch. She's officially over the dumpster fire that is her life. She needs to get off the grid, fast. Booking a secluded cabin with no cell service she hopes to get back to her dream as an artist.

James may have seemingly endless funds, but at the end of the day he doesn't have what he truly craves. After the passing of his father and a ruined past engagement, he's unconvinced love is in the cards for him. Until her. When Alexandra crashes into his life unexpectedly, she flips his world upside down.

Alexandra arrives at the cabin only to find the owner, James, still inside. With the winter storm raging and all the roads closed, they're stuck. It seems fine until the power goes out, and they're left with one bed in front of the fireplace to stay warm. The whole situation seems inconvenient, but with the snow refusing to let up and the urge to avoid James' deep questions, there's only one option for Alexandra. Distract him, no matter what she has to do.

Will they be able to stay together when they rejoin the real world and secrets are revealed?

### The Witch's Curse

Rachel's curse is nothing new. She's dealt with it her entire life. One day every year filled with bad luck.

But when Caleb, a handsome wizard ,comes to town, things start getting worse than ever before. Spilled coffee is one thing. But when her magic starts backfiring and a seers premonition looms overhead, it's time to dig deeper for a cure.

Rachel and Caleb have one day to unravel the curse, or risk it becoming worse than they could ever imagine.

### Mistletoe and Wayward Spells

Becks is overjoyed at the thought of going to Candy Cane Lane, the biggest Christmas event in the state of Massachusetts. Until the sight of mistletoe and kissing couples makes her want to use her fire magic to burn all of the tiny plants to dust.

Instead, she decides to craft a spell eradicating all mistletoe from the town. Only, the spell takes a turn and multiplies them three fold. And what's worse? The attractive tree farmer wizard informs Becks of an old town superstition. If one finds themselves under the mistletoe and refuses a kiss, they'll be cursed for eternity. Great. More curses.

### This Mess We Live In

Through the various degrees of life we experience love and pain. To be able to experience it at all is a blessing, but at times it still hurts. While new love can light you up again.

This is for the healing journey. For the fear of the unknown and how diving in can often times be the only answer.

There's brightness on the other side, you just have to keep going.

**Fade**

Ali doesn't know if she's going crazy, or if what she's feeling is real. There's a presence trying to get her attention, but what happens when she decides to believe.